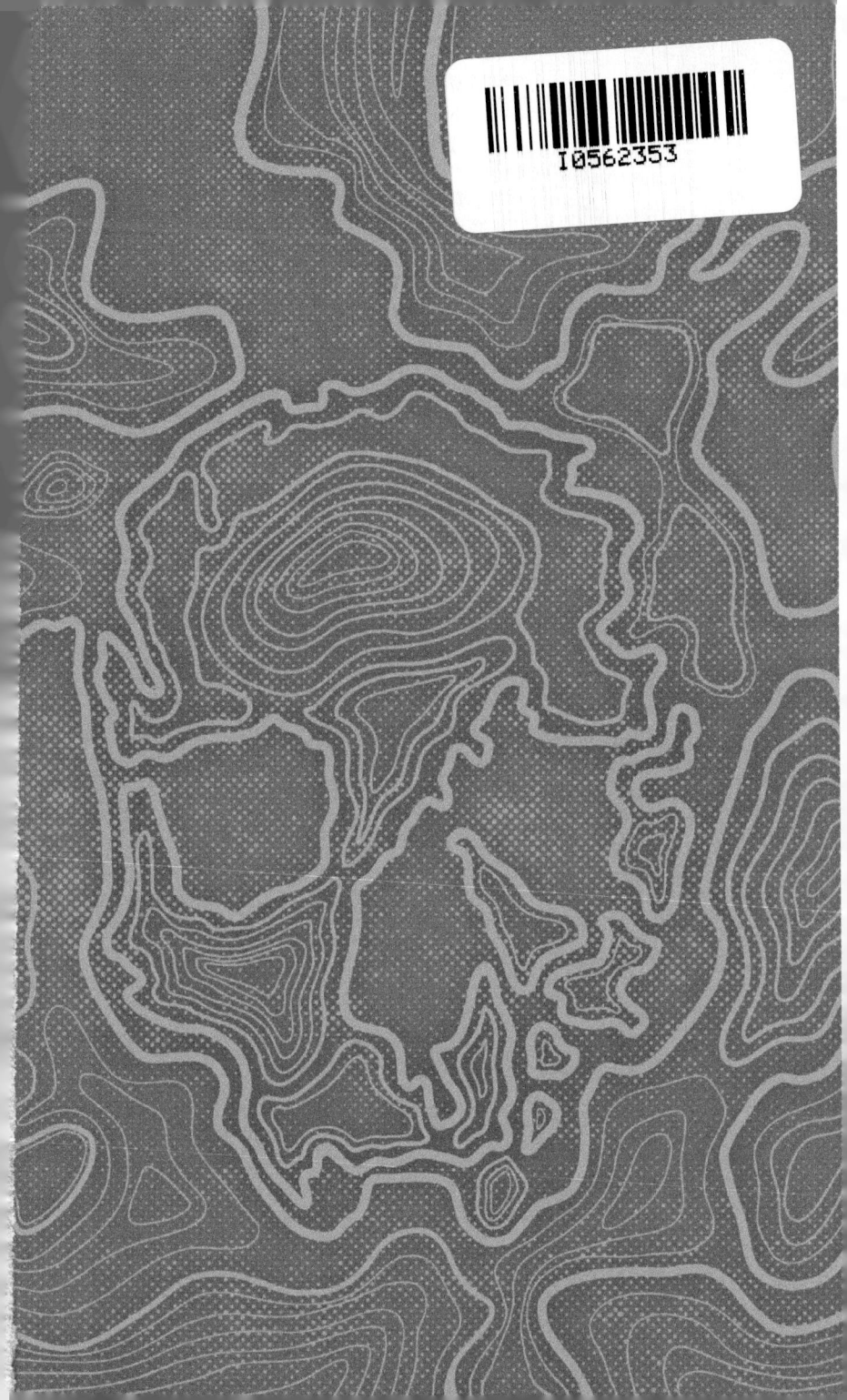

A SHORT STORY COLLECTION

NICK ORTON

Publisher: Dead Reckoning Collective
Book Cover Artwork & Design: IG: @Ram_Supply_Co
Editor: David Rose

Printed in the United States of America

Library of Congress Control Number:
2024948481

ISBN-13: 978-1-963803-09-9 (paperback)

ACKNOWLEDGEMENTS

A special thank you my family for listening to my ideas and being my first editors, and to the following individuals and organizations:

David Rose, Editor

Douglass Hoover

William "Buck" Bolyard

Levi West

Megan Mylie

The Lethal Minds Journal

The Havok Journal

The content within this book is entirely fictional and any relation to a shred of truth is nothing more than coincidental.

WHISPERS OF THE RAPTORS (FOREWORD) _____13

HUNTERS FROM THE SKY _____19

MEMORIES OF MONS _____57

THE PHONE CALL_____69

JUST A ROCK_____81

A FEAST UNSEEN IN AGES _____123

THE POINTMAN _____155

REUNION_____173

THE TAKING OF CLYDESDALE 66 _____181

THE TRANSCRIPT _____205

MAN'S BEST FRIEND _____215

LEGION OF THE DAMNED _____231

WHISPERS OF THE RAPTORS

What is it about that bump in the night that sends a cold shiver down your spine?

You know what made it. It's just a loose shutter, or maybe the heat kicking on in the basement. There's nothing scary out there—if there was, humanity would have seen it by now, right?

Catalogued it and dissected it and put its fanged maw on display in some dynamic exhibit in the Smithsonian.

It's nothing. Just the wind.

You convince yourself of that truth as you curl deeper under your covers, the light switch only feet away and cellphone held tight and at the ready.

But what if there was no light switch? What if you were out *there*, outside of the safety of your home, in the dark and surrounded by a thousand acres of trees and shadows, mountains and deserts? Huddled with your squad mates in the shallow recess of a fighting hole, each of you shivering in the icy silence that no one dares to shatter? Maybe then you'd consider the alternative—that we don't know nearly as much as we claim. That the shadows may yet hold some terrifying, blood-soaked secrets that only the dead have seen. That a mouse may never know an eagle exists until it feels the piercing grip of talons.

It's safe to say that most Americans alive now have spent nearly every night huddled in the security of their warm beds. But those who haven't, those who've spent time deep in those vast, under-explored wildernesses, or the craggy, broken cities ravaged by war and stained with hate, they know a different truth. They know that when the bump resonates through the damp night air, it's a cold reminder that humanity's position as the apex predators of this world may be little more than a comforting lie.

We fear the dark for a reason.

We are mice, and the stories you'll read here are our hushed whispers of the raptors.

Sleep tight.

— Douglass Hoover

To Sage, Sadie, and Sierra. Love you.

THE HUNTERS FROM THE SKY

PART I

The night was silent in the shadows of the Hindu Kush, save for the quiet orchestra of nature. Civilization had only dipped its toes here, barely stepping over the line. This land was feral. Winter prowled just out of reach, but a cold northern wind reminded the land that Afghanistan's winter was a guarantee. Winter was a promise, but survival was not. This was a promise the ancient denizens of these mountains understood all too well.

Dark shapes emerged from their hides and caves, scrambling out from the mountains. On hands and feet, they scrambled down the rocks and into the forests. In groups, they bounded and searched across the harsh mountain range. They dug into the soil, ripped at bark, and grabbed after unlucky souls with desperate, but determined hands.

There was much work to be done. There were many bellies to fill before the time of struggle.

Nature would have its cull come spring. In a place as desolate and rugged as this, the work needed to be done quickly, efficiently, without remorse if one wanted to survive. Instinct and memory ran the show now, all the nooks and crannies needed to be searched to fatten up with the hope for survival.

Screams and roars pierced the silence; as well as yelps of pain and calls for help. Conflict was sure to erupt in a place such as this, there were many mouths in these mountains but not nearly enough to eat. Many creatures and clans called this harsh land home, and the tyranny of scarcity forced confrontations that were a tale as old as time.

The dark shapes that searched these mountains would catch what they could, even if that meant engaging in the natural acts of violence that survival demands. Man, or beast was fair game. The night was alive with the hauntingly alien, yet familiar, sounds of whoops and chatters across the peaks, forests, and valleys.

And then, they went silent. A familiar apex predator, not of this land, had once again returned.

The two black CH-47 Chinook helicopters announced

themselves with soft rumbling and whooping as they sliced through the air. Their roar grew in intensity as they approached their final destination. They appeared out of nowhere, sweeping from the sky and diving with such speed that it seemed they were destined to crash onto the false peak that they seemed aim for. But before the collision, they reared back with such a scream it filled the valley with deafening noise. Blades kicked up a billowing cloud of dirt and dust, shielding the monsters from view.

The dark shapes that moved among the mountain lurched and ran for the cover of the darkest shadows, retreating back into their hides, lest they fall prey to these predators of the sky.

These mountains were ancient, but its denizens had long memories. This wasn't the first time the hunters from the sky stalked the land.

Before the mechanical behemoths' wheels touched the ground, the hunters inside them began to stir: awakened to action by the barks of their alphas before the dust even began to settle. The metal behemoths touched down, and the hunters ran from their maws.

The bravest of the shadows—the ones who hadn't yet fled—watched as the hunters began forming a circle, all holding their instruments of lightning and thunder. They faced out into the darkness.

Silently the hunters moved, planting their boots with the

mechanical menace of intent that had been drilled into them. After they completed their circle around the behemoths, the machines let out a mighty roar, lurching up, back up into the air.

These humans that emerged were worse than the wolves that haunted these mountains, they brought nothing but death. Some of the bolder dark shapes stole glances from cover, while others still bore the scars and memories from the last time the hunters came to stalk their prey. The dark shapes hissed and bared their teeth in silent disgust, and most certainly fear, slipping back into the shadows.

One shape remained as the others fled. It crouched behind a tree on a ridge. Its eyes peered at the hunters below. It stared intently, pondering courses of actions.

She was the oldest of her troop, a matriarch of sorts. Unlike the others she was well fed, one of the few to possess that luxury afforded as a result of her status in the troop. In her world, the strong eat first. She possessed a large stature and muscular body, all coated in dark fur. Unlike her lesser members, she was for all intents and purposes, a healthy example of her species.

Such health had awarded her long life, resisting nature's eternal call and the several attempts on her life. She snorted as she touched the scars on her chest: the wounds from her last encounter with these hunters from the sky. Some twenty years old, and they were still fresh in her mind. Her eyes narrowed as she bared yellowed fangs and a low growl escaped her lips.

Her kind were used to humans. Humans were sometimes prey. Conflict was unavoidable. Humans were simply another challenge, simply another rival and food source, presented by nature. At times the troop had overpowered the humans in the valley, but never these hunters. The troop would have to tread carefully now, but there was still work to be done. Regardless of the hunter's reintroduction to this land, the troop needed to prepare for winter.

She grunted as she turned and moved towards her hide. She crouched low, aware that her shape and size could be seen by the instruments of these humans.

But in the end it didn't really matter, these newcomers were nothing more than just... obstacles. She and her kind would do what they always had done. They would survive.

PART II

The whirring and whooping of rotors filled the night as the twin CH47 Chinooks hovered back into the sky and thundered down the valley. As soon as their black shapes vanished behind a mountain, silence filled the night.

The men were covered in darkness, but luckily for them, they owned the night. They were the elite operators of the United States Navy's SEAL Team 9.

The clear night sky was free, unviolated by modern light pollution. Petty Officer Third Class James Meldrum took in the glittering magnitude of stars as he stared through the single lens of his PVS-14 night vision goggles. The ambient light of the heavens was amplified by the 14s, revealing to Meldrum the rugged terrain of the mountains in a hazy, green hue.

This land wielded a primordial darkness that once brought fear to the primitive man. A pervasive fear that few remembered of what it meant to be prey. But with this modern wonder of technology, it was man who now lurked in the darkness. What man once feared was now held at bay by his own ingenuity.

Meldrum lay prone, pointing his M249 Squad Automatic Weapon into the darkness. He scanned from left to right, slowly taking in his "fives and twenty-fives." His infrared laser, known as a PEQ-15, further illuminated the night with a solid beam that was only visible under Meldrum's NVGs. If there was a Taliban fighter in these woods, he was ready to cut them down in a burst of 5.56.

Like many of the other Americans who now flooded into Afghanistan, James Meldrum enlisted in the Navy almost immediately after 9/11. He was a young and testosterone-fueled and wanted to fight. Sold on the legends that surrounded the SEALs, his prowess and aggression won him a contract to attend the infamous Basic Underwater Demolition/SEAL selection. Dropping out of college and some-time later freezing in the cold Pacific off a beach in Coronado, California, he cut his teeth to prove he was worthy of the almighty Trident.

Now in late 2002, here he was. After months of training, he was finally ready for a fight in this mountainous pineland that reminded him of his home in the Pacific Northwest. In fact, it was almost ominous how this foreign land reminded him of home. For a second he almost forgot where he was. For a second he was almost homesick.

Meldrum quickly snapped out of his daydream. "Get the fuck up, Meldrum," his team leader had said. He was up and falling in behind his teammates as they moved single file into the valley. His platoon was on the move.

The SEALs quickly moved through the rugged terrain; they were silent other than their footprints in the loose soil and the movement of their gear. They were keen to remain that way; they were behind enemy lines. Out here, Meldrum felt eyes on him from all angles, and the feeling they weren't alone on this remote mountain was a feeling he couldn't shake. Their enemy was ruthless and knew every tree and pebble. The men they hunted had been bred in this land; the people here that had repelled many attempted conquerors, from Alexander the Great, the British, and the Russians. Now it was the American's turn.

Meldrum was just a lowly "vanilla SEAL" in his platoon,

a newbie who hadn't been tested. This was his first mission and he understood why he was here. The SEALs were on a key leadership engagement, linking up with some local warlord interested in what the Americans had to offer and to make sure this important negotiation happened in favor of the Americans.

This was but one of many simultaneous and clandestine missions happening all over the country. Many of the Tier One assets were already tasked out to further degrade the Taliban's control on Afghanistan. While this mission was taking them deep into enemy territory, this particular warlord was sympathetic to the American dollar. Two platoons of SEALs from Meldrum's team launched from their compound on Bagram. It was evident that this mission was high visibility and of the upmost importance. Two platoons of SEALs were a significant force. However, four additional men joined them on the rumbling chinooks. Three predators in the guise of men, dragging along another who seemed more at home in a university coffee shop than in Afghanistan. .

Meldrum looked up at the two CIA operatives that led the way. The men were members of the CIA's Special Activities Division, and they were dressed in a menagerie of local garb and tactical equipment that made them look more like the Taliban than the SEALs who escorted them. The difference was the silenced MK18 carbines in their hands, and the fact that each man carried a half of a million green American dollars in their rucksacks. The additional weight didn't seem to bother them. They moved at an even faster pace than the SEALs, often slowing down to let everyone else catch up.

"These guys are like fucking cyborgs," Meldrum whispered aloud, struggling.

"Shut the fuck up," hissed Rivera, his team leader. "If you break noise discipline again," the SEAL added, "I will fuck you up."

Meldrum kept his mouth shut and his gun up. These SAD guys were something else. They would smile at you and grin, but behind those eyes, you saw something both more and less than human. The SEALs had all heard the stories. There was no doubt that these men were of the dangerous kind. These CIA types were the things that went bump in the night.

On they moved, deeper into the wildlands that seemed more and more alien. Soon the group came to a stop, the chosen location for their patrol base. It was a small hilltop with plenty of boulders and trees, and a wide view of the valley below that overlooked all approaches. More importantly, this particular spot overlooked the village and its target destination in a valley.

As the SEALs bounded to their positions, Meldrum stole a glance at the third CIA man following a few bodies behind him, the leader of the CIA team. The CIA agent only went by "Barton," and Meldrum thought he looked exactly like the crooked cop in *Training Day* with a pair of aviator glasses. He gave Meldrum the creeps, not in a perv way, but in a way that made him feel like he was locked in a room with a predator that could turn on him without warning. When Barton walked into the TOC, everyone felt the hot Afghan air suddenly go cold. No one bothered to stop or question why this plain-clothed man was suddenly standing in a secure location. He just seemed to take command of the room without saying a word.

Barton was the one who briefed Meldrum's platoon back at Bagram and made it clear that this was his operation. The operation being to sway, which was a euphemism for flat-out bribe, a local warlord to the American side of the bloodshed.

Back at the patrol base, he wore a camo pattern uniform Meldrum didn't recognize. He clutched a modified Russian RPD in one hand, while the other hand rested on their panting interpreter. In fact, Barton never let the fourth man of the CIA team, Amir, get more than a hand's reach away.

"Meldrum, get your fucking head out of your ass and pull security behind that fallen tree," barked Rivera.

Meldrum moved and set up scanning his fives and twenty-fives into the dark forest that surrounded them. He got in the prone next to the tree, taking in his fields of fire and mapping out his sectors in his head. Soon the rest of his team joined him, pointing their weapons down range. Infrared lasers streaked out into the darkness, solid beams of light cutting into the unknown. The air was silent save the wind and the whispering of the leaders behind him.

Peering into the darkness, Meldrum couldn't help but feel something was peering back. He couldn't shake the feeling that he saw something moving between the Afghan pines some hundred meters away. Meldrum stared into the wood line. Could it be some goat herder scoping them out or a Taliban scout? Or just his nerves on his first mission? Either way, something didn't feel right.

Meldrum pointed his IR laser to the spot where he thought he saw the movement, placing it right on the tree. While the naked eye couldn't see it, the IR laser lit up the spot under his NVGs. For a second he thought he saw the shape of crouched a man, slipping behind the tree. He narrowed his vision to look for any movement, maybe it was his imagination.

But it wasn't.

It happened fast, but he saw it. A head poked out from behind the tree – or something similar. It was too far away for Meldrum to see much else…but he recognized one thing: eyeshine.

He focused in on the spot now, staring intently. Two bright orbs, reflecting the infrared light of his IR laser, suddenly appeared from behind the tree. A head that had to be close to seven feet off the ground was looking out. The face was vaguely human, but not. As quickly as it appeared, the head vanished.

Meldrum was stunned; he didn't believe his eyes. Was that a gorilla? It certainly didn't look like a man.

"I think we got movement," Meldrum whispered to his team leader, who lay prone behind a boulder. "Two hundred meters north. My IR is where I last saw movement, thought it looked like a head."

Silence held as Rivera and Meldrum focused on the area illuminated by Meldrum's IR. If it was the Taliban, this operation was about to get serious. Suddenly the head reappeared; quick eyeshine and then it vanished again behind its tree.

Meldrum heard a burst of movement...moving away from them. Meldrum could see a large black shape moving out into the darkness.

"Meldrum, you're a fucking dumbass," Rivera snorted. "It's just some fucking animal. Probably smells your cherry ass. Stay focused on your sector for Taliban, not wildlife."

Meldrum got back to scanning his sectors of fire, trying to forget about what he just saw. But something didn't feel right. It looked like a man. But humans don't have eyeshine like an animal. For an eerie moment, he thought back to the legends he heard growing up in his small town about things that lurked in the wild. But Meldrum had to push it out of his mind, he had a job to do.

The rest of the night passed without incident. Eyes were peeled for the Taliban. But none ever came. The SEALs held their patrol base, fingers on the trigger all the while.

And the darkness of the night began to be painted by the faint reds of sunrise, crashing against the Hindu Kush.

PART III

"Meldrum get up, Rourke wants us at the command post." Rivera was kicking the sole of Meldrum's boot.

"Roger," Meldrum grunted, picking up his body from the cold ground. Once he'd shaken the stiffness from his bones, he began to walk up the hilltop where the patrol base had been set. All around him his fellow SEALs manned defensive positions; buddy teams spaced out in intervals and concealed in the brush and terrain. Meldrum blinked away his exhaustion. They were too far behind enemy lines to let their guard down for something like sleep the night prior.

"Meldrum, Rivera, Boone. Get the fuck over here now, you're late for the mission brief." Rourke, the second squad leader, beckoned them under some trees. The SEALs huddled with the platoon commander and team chief over a makeshift sand table. Meldrum and his team took a knee with the rest of their squad.

"Alright, eyes up and pay the attention," barked Chief Petty Officer Gimlin, a gruff and weathered man from the Deep South. "Lieutenant's going to brief you."

The platoon commander Lieutenant Patterson, began to speak. "Today there will be a key leader engagement led by the CIA team. Our mission is to provide security during this engagement. First Platoon will provide this security while Second Platoon holds this hilltop. Understood?"

"Understood," the SEALs said.

Lieutenant Patterson continued, with that Naval Academy voice of his, "We do not know the current Taliban situation, only that cells have been actively trying to recruit men to go south to fight American forces. We are here today because agent Barton will be meeting with a local warlord who may be so inclined to join the war on our side."

Patterson then pointed to the crude sand table. "This is the town of Tkah, where we will be meeting this warlord. As far as we know, the villagers are not hostile but that doesn't mean shit out here. Keep your weapons loaded and your eyes open for any aggressive intent. It's important we don't antagonize the natives, but if we need to get into a gunfight we're going to win it. ROE still applies." He paused to spit a stream of black tobacco onto the ground.

"We will enter from the main road into the middle of the town. The key leader engagement will occur in this building, the tribal elders' hut. Second squad will form a perimeter around the building and hold security. Barton, his team, myself, Chief, and Meldrum will enter the hut."

Chief Gimlin turned to Meldrum and his team. "Meldrum, you're the biggest fucker out of all of us. You got a fucking machine gun, so you get to tag along." He took a second to spit his own wad of tobacco on the ground before continuing, "Just stand there, with your mouth shut, and look scary. You got that?"

"Got it, Chief."

"Alright," Lieutenant Patterson said, "we move out in two hours. The village is about a six-mile hike from here into the valley, so get ready to walk some more. Conduct your pre-checks and be ready to move."

Once they were dismissed, Meldrum and the other SEALs began conducting gear checks. As Meldrum finally had a chance to eat something, he couldn't shake the feeling he felt last night. That feeling when looked into those trees... something was looking back at him.

PART IV

Two hours later, the SEALs and the CIA team were moving towards their objective. Second platoon stayed behind to watch the village, and for the Taliban. They were out in the wild on their own, and if it all went to hell they were their own quick response force. The patrol base held the high ground, a piece of key terrain, the small hill overlooked the village and offered a feasible fallback point to make a defensive stand or exfil.

The two agents led the way, their large rucksacks heavy with a small fortune. Regardless of the weight, Meldrum noticed again that they bounded effortlessly through the terrain. As they neared their destination, the group spread out in a "V formation" towards the village which lay near the river that bisected the valley. Meldrum stuck with the lieutenant and the chief in the middle of the "V." The CIA team was close behind them.

Soon, the forest gave way to a patchwork of fields and huts. It was evident that this village had been founded in a time that predated several generations and had been built from the mud by hand. To Meldrum it looked like a place out of time, a village that had remained the same since the wars of Alexander.

Pashtun villagers tended to meager crops and livestock but soon stopped to watch the Americans. They eyed them as they did any stranger to the village.. Outsiders, foreign or not, were to be treated with suspicion. As the SEALs approached, it was obvious to them that they weren't the first visitors. A burned-out hulk of a Russian Hind lay in a crater nearby, the rusted reminder of the past.

The SEALs and the CIA operatives collapsed into two

columns with their weapons down and at the ready; these villagers were supposed to be friendly, for now.

As the Americans walked closer to the village, what Meldrum saw left nothing to the imagination: these people were far, far detached from "modern civilization." These people and this place looked like something from ancient history, isolated from the rest of the world.

I bet these guys have no idea what's happening outside this village, Meldrum thought to himself. In fact, he was positive that running water and electricity were alien to these people. At worst, they probably considered it magic. At best, they couldn't be bothered to care for such a lack of luxuries.

The SEALs approached cautiously until they came upon a group of military-aged males. Several men of varying ages stood before them, each holding a weapon, all staring at the Americans with the same steely indifference as the other villagers. Lieutenant Patterson gave the hand signal to halt.

In the middle of the gaggle stood an old man who had to have been the village elder. Barton strode forward with Amir at his side. Meldrum listened but he couldn't understand what was being said. After a few minutes, the old man gestured to a building and started slowly shuffling towards it.

Barton turned to Lieutenant Patterson, "We'll follow the old man from here on out. He says our warlord is waiting for us. Your men will pull security as planned and we'll head inside."

The Americans followed into a small town square in the middle of the village. The group split up and headed to their respective areas. Villagers peered out through glassless windows, from around the walls of their mud huts, studying them with a skeptical caution. They didn't look like the Russians who once hunted for *Mujahideen* on these mountains, some had the wrong skin color, but Meldrum suspected they looked close enough. Afghanistan may continue to age, but some things stay the same. The SEALs were just different invaders who had the same ends as the last ones.

Second squad took their positions around the elder hut and Meldrum followed his group inside. The inside was adorned with modest cushions and rugs made by generations of women in the village. The air was warm, a stark contrast to the sharp cold air outside. But the air was heavy and musty, too, and the smell of a still-burning opium pipe pervaded the senses.

Inside they were met by a different group of men; well-fed and clothed, wearing an assortment of CHICOM and Soviet-era equipment. They carried newer rifles and held a hardened look in their eyes, a look that is only gained from someone who spends their life at war. In the middle sat another older Afghan, adorned in the same type of attire. His beard was dyed a bright orange and his skin was like wrinkled leather. He held the same sharpened stone look on his face as the younger men around him.

He must be our warlord, Meldrum thought.

The two CIA operatives dropped their rucks on the frayed carpets in front of the warlord. They opened them up and began pulling out bricks of saran-wrapped one-hundred-dollar bills; stacking taxpayer dollars on a dirty Afghan rug ready to gamble their lives. When they were done the operatives took their place on the right side of the room, weapons at the low ready. Barton and Amir approached the warlord and the cash. The warlord motioned for them to sit.

The room was small for the number of people. Gimlin and Patterson stood on the left side of the room; Gimlin motioning to Meldrum to stand by the door. Meldrum put on his best scowl, and with a M249 machine gun in hand, he knew he looked intimidating in this cramped room. If things went south, it was doubtful that anyone would get out alive.

PART V

A snow leopard crept low to the ground as it silently stalked across the Afghan wilderness. The leopard was a solitary creature, elusive as she was beautiful. Her splotchy pattern of black and tan masked her perfectly among the rock and vegetation. She spied intently a hare several bounds away, nibbling on some clover as its ears tracked any trace of noise. The leopard focused in on her meal, waiting for the right moment to strike when suddenly the hare stopped mid-meal to stare in her direction. It looked beyond her momentarily before exploding away like a spring out of sight. The leopard's fur raised as her instincts were set ablaze. She wasn't the only predator here.

The matriarch watched the snow leopard bound away from her in a flash, wisely choosing not to challenge her massive form, moving silently through the brush and foliage. Despite their size, her kind was adept at moving silently, and she made almost no sound as she shuffled behind the concealment of a large tree.

She dropped to a crouch and let out a soft hoot, just above a whisper, that was answered in kind by her mate, who remained hidden with the rest of the troop. She could smell his musk close by.

Her ears, honed by evolutions anvil, picked up the soft heartbeat of two humans nearby. Slowly, she peered around the tree trunk, carefully angling her head to reveal as little of herself as possible. Her eyes scanned the world around her, revealing details that only a predator's eye could see.

Several lengths in front of her sat two humans crouching behind a fallen log. No doubt after the same hare the leopard was. She eyed them intently: males, one old and one young. Each of them clutched those instruments of fire that the humans were fond of using.

Her ears twitched at the far-off sound of human children at play and a woman singing; they were just beyond the cover of the trees. She snorted at the filthy smell of man, decay, and waste.

The village was nearby.

It had been just under a generation since the hunters had appeared from the sky, burning half the mountain range down and hunting her kind. Even though they sought to kill their fellow humans, it was inevitable that the hunters encountered her kind. She clutched at the scars left across her chest, wounds inflicted when she was still a suckling infant by the hunters who'd aimed their fire her way.

In vain, her troop had fought them from the shadows, ambushing and consuming them just like the rest of their prey. In this world, meat was meat, and it didn't matter whose bones it came from. But those hunters had summoned their flying behemoths that spewed fire and death. Hunted by the behemoths, the *Baramou* had fled into their caves deep within the mountains.

In the darkest time of her troop's history, the *Baramou* starved, resorting to the cannibalism of the weak and useless. Even the young were not spared. Only by virtue of the troops' social hierarchy was she spared, at first, only her savagery ensured her survival to adulthood.

Only the strongest and most cunning of their kind left the safety of the mountains to later scavenge in the cover of the dark. But strife had weakened them, and many did not return as the hunters and the hunters' behemoths still prowled the mountains. It was only after the behemoths ceased to thunder did they fully reemerge.

For the next decade, they avoided humankind, having learned from their encounters. The matriarch matured, and she killed her mother to take her place as head of the troop. They ate well that night.

Under her, the troop hunted from the shadows, taking the occasional stray, and scavenged what they could. They learned to stockpile their food. In time, the troop's numbers swelled. For a short time, they prospered.

But times were ever desperate, and now the land did not provide. For reasons they didn't understand, the winters were getting longer. Colder. There were simply too many in the troop to feed. Hungry mouths and pleading hands drove the troop now.

The matriarch thought of her own daughter, starving in the safety of the cave.

She kept her eyes on the humans, feeling cold indifference for them. What came next was simply a matter of survival—a cold truth to their existence.

They desperately needed meat to fill their bellies and preserve in their caves. The village was the largest source of it within reach.

And they had the numbers. The return of the hunters

wasn't enough to dissuade them. She bellowed her command, watching the two humans jump in shock at the sudden thunder of her voice. All around her, the chatter of her troop increased in volume at once, hoots and screams piercing the quiet mountain air. Dark shapes began to move from the shadows of the forest. They didn't need to be hidden anymore.

She watched the patriarch and several males fall upon the humans with terrifying speed. The humans screamed in horror as they tried to run, the sound of fire erupting from their hands. But their fear distracted them, made them hesitate, and ultimately betrayed their will to live.

The oldest of the two raised his instrument in vain, only to be pulled from his hands and destroyed before his eyes as his face put on a mask of terror. The matriarch saw the patriarch grip both humans in his massive hands. The patriarch threw the older of the two like refuse into the forest. The matriarch watched the human stumble to his feet and flee to the village. The patriarch grasped the other male's head with his free hand, removing the human's head like a berry from the vine. He opened his mouth to drink from the fountain of sputtering blood, and the matriarch's heart fluttered as she watched him bathe in crimson before tossing the body to a group of eager youth. The patriarch scouted ahead to the village. He would feast later; there were many more humans to harvest. She refocused on the task and slipped away towards the village with the rest of her troop.

As she heard human screams erupt ahead of her, most likely caused by her mates, she briefly thought about what would happen next. She quickly shook those primitive thoughts from her head. What the future held meant little to her kind. No matter what came next, they would simply do what they had always done.

Survive.

PART VI

Amir nervously spoke a greeting on the American's behalf, but was only met with silence. He spoke the greeting again, and again was only met with silence. Meldrum could see him starting to sweat and fidget.

Chief Gimlin broke the silence in a thick southern drawl, "Aye, Amir, ask him if they got any Yetis around these parts! It's like the goddamn Himalayas up here right?"

This was only meant as a joke, an opener, a tension reliever, but Amir in his nervousness turned back from Gimlin, to the warlord, and asked him just that. Barton glared hate at the SEALs and the agents stared daggers from across the room. Meldrum thought he felt the room's temperature actually drop.

The warlord glared in a mix that appeared to Meldrum as amusement, annoyance...and anger. First at Gimlin, then

Amir.

The room was silent again, save only for the howling of the wind outside. The warlord then began to prattle on in his language. Meldrum could tell he was agitated and annoyed. He spoke a few sentences and then motioned for Amir to translate with a hurried wave of his hand.

Amir was sweating through his wool clothing; the cold sweat of a man that knew he would not survive if things did not work out as they should. He looked between the Barton and the warlord before turning his attention to First Sergeant. As he looked at Gimlin, Meldrum could feel the burning gaze of the warlord at the SEALs. He looked like he was about to have a nervous breakdown.

Amir took a breath and then stuttered: "He says he doesn't understand why you ask him this question. We are here to discuss matters that will change the fate of all the men in this room, and no matter what he will walk out with a powerful enemy, the Taliban or you."

The warlord started speaking again, and Amir on the verge of panic started to translate before Barton could interrupt.

"He says the creature you are talking about is nothing more than a beast. It's called the *Baramou*. A wild thing. A nuisance and a danger to us. When the last invaders came to this valley and their metal birds filled the sky, the *Baramou* hid in the mountains and barely survived. When the last invaders came, not only did the invaders fight us, but also the *Baramou*. Since the invaders left, the *Baramou* have returned. Yet again they steal the goats, raid the fields, scare the women and the children when they fetch water from the river. They take villagers from the fields and eat them up in the mountains. They have fought with our people for generations. He says you should know about these things already. These things are as common as the rats. He doesn't know why you ask him about these creatures when there are much more important things to discuss."

The room went silent once again. Chief Gimlin chuckled a *"what the fuck"* under his breath. Meldrum raised an eyebrow.

The warlord just confirmed that they have Yetis or whatever this Baramou is. He said they actually exist, Meldrum thought. *These people don't even have electricity; how could they know what a Yeti is unless it actually exists our here?*

Barton spoke up next and addressed the chuckling Senior Chief directly: "Shut the fuck up."

He turned to Amir, placing a stern "do-not-fuck-with-me" hand on his shoulder, and said hissed into his ear: "Let's focus and get back to work."

The negotiations continued. Meldrum remained standing for what seemed like hours watching the three-way discussion between the CIA agent, a scared shitless interpreter, and a warlord with an AK across his lap.

Meldrum couldn't tell how the negotiations were going, both Barton and the warlord held stone faces speaking to each other. Suddenly the warlord slapped his leg and spoke loudly and directly at Barton.

Meldrum felt everyone beginning to tense. Muscles began to tighten, and fingers crept tighter around trippers. Meldrum's SAW was held at the ready.

All he could hear was the silence of killers in a crowded room, and the howling wind coming from a window. Then above that wind, a howling of another kind that rose as gunshots rang out in the distance.

PART VII

Gunshots sounded in the distance as another noise rose above the wind…a noise that sent shivers down Meldrum's spine. A howl, or was it a roar? A sound alien and for some reason all too familiar for the ancestral memories deep inside Meldrum's psyche. An animalistic noise that turned his pupils into pins and his heart into a drum. Every man turned his head, toward the stone hut's window. The warlord's words mumbling then off Meldrum's lips, "Bara-mou."

The SEALs were moving.

Meldrum, Patterson, and Gimlin exited the hut; weapons at the ready. The two SAD operatives stayed behind to secure the money and hold the hut. Barton and Amir took cover outside behind a cart. The rest of the platoon had taken up positions and were pointed into the wilderness that surrounded the village.

"I need a report right now!" Lieutenant Patterson cried.

"Sir," Rivera yelled, "we heard gunshots about three hundred meters into the wood line. We received no contact; we haven't seen any Taliban or any signs of an attack. But we heard that weird ass fucking scream, sir!"

Another Seal suddenly yelled out, "I got movement, one military-aged male my twelve 'o clock; coming out of the wood line!"

The SEALs readied their weapons, could this be a suicide bomber? A Taliban scout?

"Hold your fire, hold your fire," yelled Patterson. "That's one of the villagers."

A man was sprinting up, an older man whose beard was starting to go white. Meldrum noticed right away the man's clothes were torn and he was bleeding from his scalp. His eyes were wide and panicked, he was dead sprinting at Meldrum's position before he was stopped by some other local men who wrestled him to the ground. They were yelling and speaking to him, but the man struggled and fought. He was mouthing something Meldrum couldn't make out.

Amir and Barton ran up with Gimlin and Patterson in tow. The other villagers had seemed to calm him down, but the man was blank-faced with a "thousand-yard stare" pointed straight ahead. He whispered something to Amir who after paused in confusion and asked him again a series of questions. Amir stood up, confused, turning to the others with fear in his eyes.

"He said...he said he and his son were hunting in the woods. *They* attacked them. *They* killed his son and dragged him away."

"What do you mean *they*?" Barton demanded.

Amir repeated what the man said, adding, "I don't know, he called it a monster. There was a group of them, they were big and whatever they were, they almost grabbed him. They were ambushed, and he said when he fired his gun, one grabbed his rifle and snapped it in two before, before—"

"Before *what*?" Barton growled.

"Before they ripped off his son's head...like a chicken."

"Bullshit. Has to be Taliban. This guy's lost it." Gimlin started eying the wood line. He spat.

Suddenly, shrill screams rang out. Everyone looked up, and Meldrum's eyes grew wide. A group of children fled from the wood line and the horrible wail of a woman filled the air as they ran back to the village.

Just past the edge of trees, a woman was being ravaged: beaten by a man who lifted her up and slammed her body on the ground.

No, Meldrum thought. *That's no man.*

"What the fuck is *that*!" a SEAL called out.

It was taller than a man. Draped in fur, it swung its hauntingly human eyes off the woman at its feet and onto the village. It stared at them with an uncanny intelligence. No man there had a chest so wide or shoulders that broad, or muscles that bulged under thick black, brownish hair. Meldrum thought back to the legends of his youth.

"There's no fucking way," someone said.

"Is," Meldrum yelled, "Is that fucking *Bigfoot*?!"

Part VIII

The creature or whatever it was, placed its foot on the struggling woman. Meldrum could hear ribs break as she screamed in pain. The beast placed its weight on her chest as it reached down and gripped her arm, ripping it off in one sickening twist. The creature then tore into the arm with its teeth, chomping down on the tender flesh.

The creatures' eyes never removed themselves from the men: it sized them up with growing malice and challenge. With a mouthful of flesh, it began to grunt and hoot. Dropping the arm, it began to beat its chest. It screamed horribly. Meldrum swore he could feel his chest reverberating with its roar. As if summoned by the scream, more dark shapes began to emerge from the wood line.

The Afghans had retreated into their huts in a controlled

panic. They barricaded themselves and huddled behind cover as the men pointed rifles with shaking hands at the doors and windows, praying that it wasn't their hut chosen. Only the Americans remained in the open to face the *Baramou*.

Meldrum scanned left to right; more tall figures emerged from the cover of the dark forest. There must have been twelve to fifteen of them now stepping out into the open, but Meldrum could see more shadows hanging back deeper in the woods. The newcomers resembled the first creature that still stood over the body of the woman. However, these creatures were shorter and less muscular; they looked almost emaciated compared to the big one. Some held rocks and others makeshift spears, all of them bearing their large fangs, and all of them moved towards the village.

The tall one, the obvious leader of this troop, began to shift its screaming; sounding more like a gorilla and the wailing of a banshee. The others followed suit, beating their chests, joining in with the same screams. Meldrum's ears rang, and his trigger finger itched.

"Sir, what are your orders?" a team leader laying in the prone yelled. The SEALs had their guns up and ready.

"Hold fire, hold fire!" Patterson shouted back. He turned to Barton, "Do you know what the fuck this is?"

Barton kept his eyes on the creatures and kept Amir behind cover. "The intel didn't cover this, Lieutenant. But if I was a betting man, I'd bet think these things aren't here to win hearts and minds."

The creatures were foaming at the mouth. They shook fully grown trees like they were saplings. Some smacked the ground with both hands generating a sound like a gunshot. The younger ones had tasted human blood and their empty stomachs demanded more. Others remembered the *Hunters From The* Sky and were eager to chase them off the mountain again.

Rocks were being tossed now, baseball and basketball sized stones that could easily kill a man. Some landed on the huts and a few amongst the Americans, closely missing a few surprised SEALs. But the SEALs still held their fire and watched their heads. Unsure of how to proceed they still kept their fingers on the trigger, but didn't engage.

The tallest of the creatures beat its chest and let out a final roar. Blood frothed from its mouth. Its fangs bared like yellow stained daggers and a geyser of hot breath spewed forth into the cold mountain air. Then it charged. Its muscles rippled as it thundered towards the SEALs.

Then its brethren followed.

"Oh shit," yelled a SEAL, "here they come!"

The SEALs all saw how easily the creature had torn that arm off that woman. Like pulling a leaf from a tree. They didn't doubt that if one of those things got close enough, they would suffer the same fate.

Meldrum could see the whites of the creatures' eyes now closing in. Now they looked a little more human; an ape and Neanderthal mix; something out of a textbook. Those eyes carried a little more intelligence now, a little more fear, a whole lot of savagery.

Some *Baramou* ran on two legs, others hunched over in a horrid gallop. The creatures' mouths were open, four dagger-like fangs flashing yellow in the cold mountain air. They were getting closer.

Lieutenant Patterson shouted, "Open fire!"

PART IX

Meldrum had already picked his target, the tallest of the creatures now stomping towards him. Kneeling behind a low wall, he lined up his optic center mass on the leader; maybe a hundred feet away. Its great size made target acquisition easy. Meldrum wasn't sure what the goal of the creature's charge was, not that he had time to care. His finger slowly depressed the trigger, and his M249 came to life.

A hail of 5.56 spewed from his barrel. Red blossoms began to burst across the chest of the *Baramou*, resulting in a bellowing of rage.

What the 5.56 NATO round lacked in mass and stopping power, the SAW made up for in volume. Meldrum had a one-hundred-round "pork chop," and he intended to use it.

The lead *Baramou* was getting closer, and Meldrum shifted his fire to its lower body. The M249 machine gun lived up to its moniker, "the SAW," cutting the creature down at the legs. Hot led shredded the soft tissue below the creature's waist. The rounds shattered bone and cut through flesh.

The creature fell face-first in the dirt, collapsing into a tangle of limbs. It tried to pick itself up, struggling, fighting through wounds that would have killed any man. It struggled back to its feet, it was so close now that Meldrum could hear its blood now beginning to gurgle in it's throat.

As the creature moved to continue its attack, Meldrum let out a burst to its upper torso. The doomed creature absorbed the rounds in its neck and face, turning it into a mess of blood and gore.

The creature finally fell, but Meldrum fired another burst for good measure.

"Die mother fucker," he whispered.

He fished out another pork chop and reloaded. More shapes were closing in and he let the SAW rip.

The *Baramou* were used to their numbers working to their advantage. Their savagery allowed them to overcome the meager attempts the humans of this valley threw at them. Even the previous hunters from the sky had fallen to their savage attacks and ambushes from the darkness. Brutality, surprise, and fear were their weapons against the humans they wielded with terrifying effectiveness. But in this instance, those weapons fell short. The creatures had miscalculated.

Around Meldrum, other SEALs made short work of the attack. Those that didn't have an M249 quickly dispatched the other creatures by the time-honored strategy of shooting them in the face. Once the bodies hit the ground, the rest of their magazines followed in quick succession. *Baramou* began to lay crumbled and motionless in the early afternoon sun.

Those that remained began to turn and run. As they fled, the SEALs sent more rounds their way. They began to seek cover behind the trees, still hooting and screeching. Some of the *Baramou* dragged their dead and dying off, into the cover of the forest.

"Ceasefire!" shouted Lieutenant Patterson. "Ceasefire!"

The SEALs let off their triggers and changed magazines. From behind the trees, angry eyes peeked and hungry mouths hung open. The hoots and hollering sounded like a troop of panicked monkeys.

"Hit that tree line with 203's, suppressive fire into that tree line!" shouted Patterson.

Four distinct *thumps* sounded and a second later 40mm grenades exploded and the fight was over. With a kill radius of fiver meters per, anything not killed by the explosions got peppered with metal fragments and shrapnel. Meldrum and the other M249 gunners let loose into the forest, sending over suppressive fire in the form of a wall of lead.

Shouts of "Cease fire" began again.

Silence on the mountain took over as the SEALs scanned ahead. Barrels smoked and blood was beginning to be absorbed by a parched ground.

The SEALs walked cautiously to the tree line. Gunshots rang out as the SEALs made sure all the bodies were truly dead.

"I think we go them all. Think they ran off." Meldrum mused to one of his teammates as they surveyed the carnage. As he walked up to a new body, he saw it was still breathing. The creature looked at him with a mix of feral rage and fear. It began to move, lashing out towards him with furious, desperate hands. If this was a horror movie, Meldrum was sure the creatures would have killed most of them, with only one of them left standing after a night of sheer terror. Meldrum fired a burst into the Baramou's torso.

"This isn't a movie," he said to himself.

The warlord exited the hut with his entourage, staring wide-eyed at all the bodies still bleeding out on his soil.

Barton stood up with Amir and walked up to him. Barton turned to Amir and said, "Tell him: Are we ready to make a deal?"

A MEMORY OF MONS

From the memoirs of COL (ret) Michael Raeford

As of writing this memoir, I am of eighty-nine years of age and I have lived an excellent life, documented by my hand upon these pages. While most has already been written, I have decided to end things with the following confession, a confession of an event that has forever haunted me.

I will take you back, once again, to the conflict I simply remember back then as "The War." It was August 31, 1944, back when I was a young non-commissioned officer in the 3rd Armored Division on our drive across Europe.

We had thrust into Belgium and were closing in on a large force of Waffen SS and Wehrmacht soldiers. The Allies had been pushing the Germans back, and as luck would have it, we managed to push Army Task Group Straube into a corner in what would later be known as the "Battle of the Mons Pocket." The Germans were battered and bruised, and our generals smelled blood. We would attempt an encirclement and force the Germans to surrender or we would blow them all to hell!

It was there that I found myself, a young platoon sergeant, given the task of leading some fifty-odd soldiers into battle. We were a mixed batch, made up of "old breed" such as myself, and fresh recruits off the boats. Our task was to assault into that town of Mons; a formerly sleepy little hamlet in the Belgian countryside.

While we were told the Germans were disorganized and demoralized, we still faced some 70,000 of them, almost all from the 5th Panzer Division, still holding the line. The way they had already savaged the initial attacks on Mons told us all we needed to know about their desire to fight.

The night before the battle, I laid awake. The Germans may have been on the run, but that made them that much more dangerous. I remembered from my youth what happens when you corner a wolf. The Germans would fight savagely to stop us from advancing, as the Rhine lay a few days away, and beyond that the Fatherland itself.

I laid there feeling that many in my company, myself included, would not survive. After all the killing and death I had seen from Africa to Italy, I could only imagine myself dying in a pool of my own blood, wrapped in my own guts, in Belgium dirt, after a burst from a Kraut's machine gun.

A heavy blanket of dread fell over me, and I found myself doing something my pride at that time would never admit to: I prayed. I must confess at that time I was not a deeply religious man; I had always considered myself an atheist in the foxhole. I had seen enough death to last a man ten lifetimes. I simply felt that if prayers were being heard in this terrible period, God and his angels must be deaf.

Nevertheless, I found myself reciting what my mother had begged me to memorize: a prayer to St. George, the patron saint of the Army.

I did so deeply that night, several times. My dread was soon replaced by a strange comfort. I like to think that it was just self-acceptance, but the events that followed would make me believe my prayers had been answered.

We mustered early that next morning, the air smelled of diesel and freshly churned mud as sherman tank engines droned like war drums all around. Artillery fire had begun in earnest to rain steal upon the Germans just out of sight. We began our slow march to our assault positions. German artillery began in earnest. We crouched behind trees and shrubbery, anything to conceal us as we overlooked Mons. I could see gray and black shadows darting about far below. The downwind carried the now whispers of Germans yelling in our ears. They sang songs full of defiance, demanding that their bodies form a bulwark against us.

Again, the wave of despair flowed, into my mind as well as the minds of my men around me. We huddled low behind cover. We sank, a little deeper into the earth, and we flinched a little harder at the artillery that whistled overhead.

I could feel my death down there. We all could.

It was oppressive, this feeling that descended on us. Despite our progress, it felt as if we would fail here. Almost like clockwork, our artillery began to increase. Normally, this would have been encouraging. But not this day. If the Germans didn't know we were about to attack, they did now.

I found myself whispering that prayer to St. George. The men around me heard my whispers and asked to join. Soon, the lot of us were praying to whom we barely believed in, to a God we had doubts even existed. But soon as the order was given to prepare to advance into Mons we stopped praying. This was it, the moment had come.

The Shermans lurched forward, their cannons bellowing in challenge to the Germans beyond. A lieutenant looked at me and gave the order to advance. We leaped up from our hiding places and began to follow behind. The Germans began to send a hail of fire our direction, and soon the one Sherman we had been using for cover took a direct hit. It went up in a chilling inferno and we hit the ground as bullets whizzed overhead. Not all of us were fast enough, though, and the lieutenant took a bullet to the face, spilling blood all over my own. The noise was deafening, and terrifying, and then something stood out among the cacophony. A whistle.

It was a shrill and sharp. First one long blow, then several in a quick succession. Then the roar of several men yelling all at once. I looked up from the grass behind me to see a peculiar sight. Riflemen! Reinforcements, thank God! But then it dawned on me, they had seemingly appeared from thin air! They were coming up from behind us, which was odd, as there was no other unit there. There were no reserves to come to our aid, no new troops to be counted on. I noticed also that they were equipped differently, and their voices sounded, of all things, British.

These riflemen ran forward, beckoning us to get up and follow, firing and cycling their bolt action rifles at the Germans. One lad brandishing a revolver ran up to me, grabbing my arm, bringing me to my feet and exclaiming, "Come on, Sergeant, the Hun isn't going to wait for us!"

I was beside myself. The man seemed to glow, as if a soft light emanated from his skin. He seemed almost translucent, ghostly even. Then the wind changed, stoking the tank's flames and the fire cast a different light on him. Before me was a decaying corpse. I'm sure I gave him a ghastly stare. The officer slapped my shoulder and gave me a jolly shake, saying with a sly grin, "You look like you've seen a ghost, lad."

He ran ahead of me and I snapped out of my shock to give the order for my men to rise up and follow. The risen dead men moved quicker than us, almost floating over the ground. Bullets and shrapnel seemed to have no effect on them, I never saw a single one of them fall or flinch. But I saw the Germans growing frantic.

The undead riflemen converged their assault to a single location, and we followed closely behind. They were going to force a breakthrough of the German lines! While the German weapons had no effect on them, I witnessed Germans gunned down by rifle fire so accurate, our own volume could not compare. Once the riflemen broke the lines, they quickly got to work with their bayonets and the butts of their rifles. I witnessed a Kraut in horror pinned to the ground, run through by a ghostly bayonet, its wielder having been shot point blank to no effect.

Our ghostly saviors pushed forward into the town, but by the time we had arrived at the first defenses...they were cleared. They had vanished ahead, leaving dead and terrified Germans in their wake. As we pushed, we discovered more and more dead, all German, each with a look of pure terror put on them in their final moments.

As we caught up with our ethereal reinforcements, the riflemen vanished in a bright and sudden flash. With more fighting and ground to take, we couldn't dither. We had a town to take. And take it we did.

After that day at Mons, we encircled the Krauts. They were disorganized and demoralized and finally broken. Even the Waffen SS held their heads low in and their hands high in the air. Even more amazing is we only lost 89 of our own souls in exchange for 3,500 of theirs. Over 45,000 Germans would be taken prisoner and countless pieces of their equipment were captured. The remaining Germans decided they couldn't hold northern France and Belgium; they turned their tail and ran to hide behind the Siegfried Line. So easy was it to break the resolve of the enemy that we once had to smash with tooth and nail to push them back but a mere few steps. It seemed biblical how we suddenly overcame them. Maybe it was.

Unfortunately, the exploits and events of those days were overshadowed by bigger, more decisive engagements. The mysterious happenings of that battle were discussed often in the days that followed. However, talk of "ghosts" soon faded to obscurity, we had to focus on not catching a Kraut bullet and becoming ghosts ourselves. We rolled across Europe and into the heart of Germany herself, never seeing them again.

I rose through the ranks after Mons. Perhaps it was luck or perhaps it was skill. I like to think that my good fortunes were at the cost of the poor fortunes of better men.

Regardless, I found myself a young officer by battlefield

promotion by the end of the war. By the time the Russians had raged into Berlin, the war in Europe was over. But war was still raging elsewhere, and the fight was not yet done. I found myself transferred back to London, attached to a quartermaster unit overseeing the transfer of equipment and soldiers to the Pacific Theater.

I confess I had pushed the events that happened at Mons into the back of my mind by the war's end in 1945. Such is the result of trying to survive.

But then one day, I strolled into a pub off the beaten path to drink my thoughts away. It was there that I came across a British lad in full dress, a soldier by the name of Patrick Johns. The drunken bastard was already several pints drowned, but upon seeing me in my own uniform, he shouted in joy and beckoned me over. I can still hear his cockney accent, "Oi, Yank! Come let me buy you a drink!"

And so, we struck up a barside friendship that only a war and strong drinks can bring.

We began to regale in our drunken excitement the war stories, hostage the bar was to our tales! It turned out he was a paratrooper who took a crash landing at Arnhem. His time in his army was now limited to maintaining weapons and blowing his paycheck at any pub he could crawl into. It was a jolly encounter, I had not laughed and smiled as much as I did that night in ages. The beer was helping me remember things I'd forgotten (or, more plausibly, pushed mightily down).

Johns' mood shifted once I began talking about Mons.

Once I mentioned the strange events of that day, he suddenly seemed to sober up and his voice became a whisper. He asked me to retell the story, again and again, each time asking for more details about the riflemen. Pestering me about every little nuance I could remember. Getting slightly perturbed, I finally asked why he was so interested.

He proceeded to tell me that his father, an officer in the British Expeditionary Force, fought in the Great War against the Huns at Mons. His father would later tell his son about an incredible incident during the battle. And as Johns began to dive deeper, I felt the freezing of my blood.

He spoke how his father under the steel rain of artillery, made preparations with his men to "go over the top" and storm the German trenches. It surely meant death for many of the men in the trench who readied themselves. Johns' father in dire need of divine protection began to recite a prayer to Saint George. Hearing him, his men began to recite the prayer as well. The prayer ended as the whistle was blown and the men began their mad dash over the trench into no man's land.

But instead of a hail of German bullets, the soldiers witnessed bowmen firing arrow after arrow into the German lines. They were English longbowmen. Johns' father called them angelic. And they rained a devastating volley on the

German lines. Arrows that seemed to be made out of nothing pierced Kraut hearts with deadly accuracy. John's father and his men stormed the trenches, fighting side by side with these ghostly archers. When the Germans were pushed from the trench, Johns' father said they vanished in a flash of light. Other soldiers would witness a similar event unfold across the front.

John's father claimed they were English longbowmen from the Battle of Agincourt called back to earth as angels to fight on the fields once more. To those who witnessed them, they became known as the "Angels of Mons."

I sat there flabbergasted, then I began my own questioning. Johns' father had spoken little of the war, other than the incredible events that happened at Mons. He had survived the "War to End All Wars" only to be later killed during Hitler's damn Blitz. So many questions were left unanswered. But Johns was adamant that his father believed he witnessed angels fighting.

Breaking through my shock, I remembered the ghostly officer who'd waved us forward. The bastard's face was seared into my memory, having been pushed deep down or not. And a part of me had known it all evening: I was staring at the face of his son.

Our time together came to an end. We embraced as brothers and soon parted ways as strangers in our own stories. I never did see Johns again. But I soon became obsessed with finding answers to explain what I saw at Mons. Not surprisingly, there was not much to find.

Over the years, I found scraps of writing and articles that detailed the Angels of Mons, ghostly archers appearing to turn the tide of a battle over trenches. Vague accounts and dubious conjecture. Just a strange footnote of the First World War. I never found a single mention of my own experience, and not many of the surviving members of my unit who were there that day were eager to discuss the topic. I would never regain contact with my former compatriots. I kept my story close to my heart, and I felt no one could believe the story that I had. I would be considered a charlatan! An invalid! The war had robbed me of my sanity! Ha! Maybe it had!

This leaves me with this final entry. A secret I've held close to my heart. I am now eighty-nine years of age. I have lived a good life and dammed if I am to be judged now.

In my quiet studies, I could never find an explanation of what I saw that day. At worst, it was a hallucination or a hoax. But that day changed me. I had begun to consider the world in a new light: at best it was a miracle, and an act of God intervening in the despicable world of men.

But one thing haunted the back of my mind, and still haunts me, even now in the twilight of my life. Johns' father witnessed archers from Agincourt. I, in turn, witnessed his father and his men from the First Great War.

When the time comes to defend Mons once again, will I be called back from the realm of the dead? Shall I be expected to hold my rifle one more time?

Will I be among the next Angels of Mons?

THE PHONE CALL

It was the Saturday morning of an otherwise forgettable long weekend in Oceanside, California. Many of the Marines and Sailors of Camp Pendleton had decided to kick things off with copious amounts of alcohol; and in the early morning, many were crawling back into their barracks room beds to sleep off the hangovers.

However, Martin "Marty" Finnegan had long retired from weekend benders. At this moment, he had been fast asleep next to his wife. Had been, because the sound of a buzzing cellphone next to his head ripped him from his blissful realm.

He cracked his eyes and squinted in the darkness. The

clock read 0302. Too goddamn early. Half asleep he turned and reached to grab his phone, preparing himself for the revelation of some shenanigans that his Marines had gotten into. Shenanigans that he would have to deal with personally.

"Who's calling, hun?" whispered his wife, annoyed. She didn't even open her eyes.

Martin's eyes burned as they adjusted to the blinding light of the screen. The name "Hayden Attoway" was displayed.

He sighed a breath of relief. No first sergeant was telling him to pick up a Marine from the local drunk tank. "It's Hayden," he whispered. "Sorry to wake you up, babe. I'll go take this out back."

"It's ok, just *please* don't wake the baby," Jenny said. His newborn daughter started to stir and coo in annoyance in the bassinet next to her mother.

He quickly denied the call and texted Hayden: *Hey man give me a second. Lemme call you right back.*

Martin rolled out of bed and closed the phone screen. Stepping carefully, he crept past his daughter. As he walked out of the room, he stole a glance behind him. Both mom and baby were back fast asleep. Crisis averted.

He shuffled through their house towards the backyard. He grabbed a beer from the fridge on his way outside. *Fuck it. I'm not working today, it's Memorial Day. Might as well*, he mused. The Marine Corps had fried any ability for him to go back to sleep after being jolted. The baby would soon be up anyways. Nothing coffee and nicotine couldn't later fix.

As he shuffled to the back patio, he was already planning out the day's events: watching football and grilling meat in the California sun while killing the thirty pack in his fridge. Well, twenty-nine pack. Between sips, he tripped over his boots he'd thrown on the ground to air out when he had come home on Friday. He picked them up and carried them back inside to the closet in the laundry room where he kept all his uniforms, dropping them next to a pile of dirty cammies and silkies. He paused to make sure the girls were still asleep before trying his best to creep back to the patio.

Martin paused when he caught a glance at a clean uniform hanging in the closet, focusing on the three chevrons and a rocker that adorned the collar. It seemed like yesterday he was a boot walking nervously into his first unit. But now, 2007 seemed ages ago, and he wasn't a boot anymore. Martin took another sip and headed out to the back yard.

The dark early morning was quiet and cool. If he tried he could almost hear the waves; perks of living in Camp Pendleton's Del Mar housing.

He opened his phone and wondered why Hayden had called so late. Then again, it wouldn't be the first time. Usually it meant he needed to go grab him because Hayden' project motorcycle crapped out somewhere in Fallbrook. But usually a late night call was Hayden just wanting to drunkenly bullshit over the phone. Any time he called; Marty always obliged. What are best friends for?

Martin and Hayden had been best friends for a while, the Corps and war had forged them into brothers. Which was hilarious considering at one time Hayden had been his team leader and hazed the then boot Martin relentlessly when he joined the fleet in 2007. It wasn't until Martin choked Hayden out in a bout of "combative reconditioning," did he elevate himself from "piece of shit" to one of the guys. Hayden had reluctantly accepted him before offering to share cigarettes with Martin at the smoke pit. Martin had been part of the brotherhood ever since.

Martin hit call and raised his phone. "Hey man, what's up? You good?"

"Maaarrrtty, it's me Hayden," slurred Hayden on the other end. It sounded like he was still drinking the previous night away. Not surprising, knowing Hayden.

"Dude, what's up? You good? Where you at?"

"Yeah man, I'm fine, and I decided to party at home this weekend. Just me, myself, and I."

"Well what's up? It's like 0300, too, man. I haven't heard from you for a while."

"Yeah, my bad man. Been busy, you know? Just wanted to have some alone time. You know how it goes."

Martin felt a little guilty. Even though he considered Hayden his best friend, they'd grown a little distant recently. He'd been caught up being a new dad, and hadn't found the time to spend with Hayden like he used to. Hayden had his own family and had been moved to another unit on Camp Horno. Martin hardly saw him unless it was on the odd weekend. The two inseparable friends suddenly found themselves quite apart.

"Yeah man," Martin said. "I know how it goes. I've been shitty at communicating too, man."

"Shit sucks since Betty left with the kids," Hayden slurred through the phone. "But what can I do?" Martin thought he heard a sob.

"Shit, man, I'm... I'm sorry to hear that." Martin was caught off guard, he knew that Hayden and Betty were having issues, but he didn't know she'd left! He realized it had been longer than "a minute." He felt pretty shitty considering the two worked on the same base and lived only twenty minutes apart. It suddenly made Martin's heart ache and his beer taste sour.

"It's whatever, man. It's whatever. But...I wanted to ask you a question, Marty."

Hayden was happy to change the subject, mainly to get his mind off his building guilt. "Yeah, man. What's going on?"

"Do you remember Jake?"

Martin paused; he hadn't thought about the missing member of their trio in a while either. Jacob Hayes was their friend and former squadmate. The three of them used to be inseparable. Best friends. Brothers. He was killed on their first deployment to Iraq. Like all friends' deaths, Jake's was hard to move on from. And maybe that was why Martin's mind had eventually chosen to do something like forger.

"Yeah, man. I remember Jake," Martin said regretfully.

"You remember how he died?" Hayden asked.

Martin again paused. As much as he wanted to forget, he couldn't. He had been there when it happened. Their platoon was conducting a patrol in Ramadi, practically look-ing for a fight with whatever Iraqi wanted to kill them that day. The streets were quiet besides the wind and the Marines footfalls. Martin remembered how he clutched his M16 as he watched for movement in dark windows and obscured alleyways. They had been in country for a few months and were well accustomed to the dangers of the raging insur-gency.

It happened when they entered a bazaar. Hayden was on point when they halted just inside the tents and booths. The people were eerily absent, looking like they simply dropped what they were doing and disappeared. There was even food left; half eaten, and on the ground. Jake volunteered to take point when the Marines started moving again, striding out in front of Hayden as they walked further into the bazaar. Jake Hayes had been the first to welcome Martin into the tribe, and the man who brought Martin and Hayden together. Three amigos. He was a man who smiled in the face of an otherwise cruel world, strong enough to be gentle. Jake Hayes was a natural born Marine who was no better friend in war. He was a man who seemed like he would survive all that combat could throw at him. The last Martin and Hayden had saw of Jake Hayes alive was him engulfed in a geyser of fire. He had stepped on an IED. In one instant all that was left of Jake was a mangled body and a shattered rifle.

Martin took a long swig, it was sour now and burned his throat. He said plainly, "Yeah, man. I do." Martin's eyes were looking back into a place far away. A place in another time. A place that was nothing but painful memories.

"My memory's fuzzy, man," Hayden said. "You know, from that big IED in Ramadi, I... I can't remember."

"Hayden, I really don't want to talk about this." Jake Hayes' end was something he would rather not retell. It was the one out of the many that haunted him most. Jake Hayes was denied a clean death. Denied an honorable death. He'd died brutally. Blasted to pieces by an IED planted by a kid for twenty dollars. Eviscerated into something that no longer resembled a man. He died in some shitty bazaar, on some shitty patrol, in some shitty war that most Americans didn't give a shit about.

"Yeah," Hayden stuttered, "but do you remember what happened afterwards? After he died?"

Martin paused. This was something he also didn't want to revisit. Jake's death had haunted him, but what had come after had unsettled Martin to this day.

"…Marty?"

Martin mulled it over, gulping down the last of his beer. He sighed, "I remember we saw him again, on that convoy outside Ramadi."

Hayden's voice changed, "I remember now, we saw him standing in the middle of the road. Clear as day. You slammed on the brakes stopping the whole convoy. LT came on the net cussing us out for that." Martin could hear Hayden softly chuckle on the other end.

"We were the only ones who could see him, our gunner kept telling us how he couldn't see anything. But we saw him there, pointing to a spot on the road." Martin breathed in, heart beginning to race. "Pointing to that fucking pressure plate IED that would have sent us all to hell."

"And after that we, we saw him everywhere."

Martin sighed, "Hayden why are we talking about all this?"

"Jake saved our lives, right?" Hayden blurted. "He saved our asses! Remember how we would see him pointing towards all those other IEDs? We always found them, too. He would stand right next to them, just pointing."

Martin started to get upset, "But only we could see him, remember? We almost got pulled from the unit because of it. We were losing it. Jake's death traumatized us. It was all in our heads."

"Bullshit! Bullshit, Martin! You know that's bullshit! That's not what you told me over there, that's not true. That's not what we *believed*. What did we really think it was!?"

Martin sighed again, "I remember that we believed that it was his ghost. That he came back from the dead to warn us, to keep us alive." Tears were coming down his eyes.

Martin heard sobbing from the other end of the phone, deep and painful sobs.

"I should have died there man, in Iraq." Hayden now cried like a child. "I. Should. Have. Died. Not Jake. All that death, and I'm still alive. I got to come home. I couldn't get right. Couldn't be that Good Marine. Couldn't do shit for my family. I don't know why I'm here anymore." Martin heard his friend repeat over and over, "I'm sorry."

"Hayden." Worry was welling up inside of Martin. He prayed his friend would stay on the phone while he figured out what to do.

"He's here, man. Jake is here in the house with me. He's been here all day, and I don't know what he wants."

"What?!" There was only silence on the phone now. Martin tried several things, to get his friend to talk again, for one, maybe even get him to make a semblance of sense. But there was nothing now, save for a burst of frantic sobs and then the line went dead.

Martin was moving. Hayden wasn't far and he didn't have time to lose. He jumped into his car and peeled out of the driveway. He had already lost one of his friends, but tonight he wasn't going to lose another one. He called 911 as he sped through the early morning streets of Oceanside, pulling up to his Hayden' house as he told the operator his friend was in crisis. He blurted out the address before bolting from his still-running car.

He frantically knocked and slammed on the door. He yelled for Hayden to open the hell up. Nothing. He had to find another way in. He started brainstorming breaking a window as he began to kick the door. Then, and it was so crisp and clear the sound stayed him, the tell-tale "thunk" of a lock slid and then stopped. The door was now unlocked.

Martin grabbed the handle and burst into the house, expecting Hayden to be standing there...but the doorway was empty. *I must have not realized the door was unlocked,* Martin told himself. He saw the shape of a man walk away; into the dark home. He called out to Hayden as he ran inside. He was oblivious to any danger, he just wanted to get to his friend.

The place was a mess, beer cans and trash lay everywhere. It wreaked of old cigarettes and older food. Hayden was a neat freak, and to see his house in this condition must have meant he was really going through it. Martin also noticed the house was practically empty. Betty was gone.

Martin felt that guilt hit him like the insurgent's round he'd taken to the chest. Had he really not bothered to check on his friend?

He moved into the living room, calling Hayden's name. And it was there he froze in place with his eyes wide.

On the sofa sat Hayden. A meager coffee table held several empty liquor bottles. Pills lay spilled and scattered. Hayden was still crying; one hand wrestling with a handgun. Martin's eyes were drawn to the *other* hand that wrestled with Hayden, holding back the gun as best it could as the weapon inched closer and closer to Hayden' head. And who that other hand belonged to. Martin was in pure disbelief, but his hair sure believed it; standing on end as a chill ran down his spine.

He wore a pair of desert cammies, clean and crisp. Jacob Hayes, intact as he'd been before that malicious IED, stood to the right of Hayden as he grappled with the handgun.

"Not today, Hayden." Jacob Hayes, a dead man, said aloud. His other hand was placed on Hayden' shoulder. "Not like this."

Martin felt goosebumps as Jacob turned his gaze. "Look, Martin is here. It's going to be okay, dude. Martin is here."

Hayden also turned towards Martin. His eyes were filled

with a pain that overflowed into Martin's heart. As he looked away, the sobs of a broken man shook Martin to his core.

At that moment Lance Corporal Jacob Hayes, killed by an IED in Iraq, gently took the handgun away. Hayes cupped Hayden' head with his free hand and embraced him. "I'll see you again, man. But when it's your time."

Jacob Hayes then walked towards Martin, who was still absolutely frozen. Hayes placed a hand on his shoulder and shoved the gun into his hands. He hugged Martin too, and he felt as real as the day he'd died. Martin wished it would last forever, but Jake pulled away and Martin thought his heart would break all over again.

"I'm always here," Jacob Hayes said to both of them. "Don't wait for me." He began to vanish. "Live your life. I'll see you again."

JUST A ROCK

PART I

The cool tropical night was coming to an end as the rising sun marked the beginning transition to the new day. The blackness of the sky was replaced slowly with an ominous red glow, like lava spewing forth into the sky. The sun slowly rose over the city of Hilo and with it the familiar tropical heat as the sun took its place high above the Big Island of Hawaii.

The roads weren't yet filled with commuters going about their day and tour busses crammed with chatty tourists emerging out of there cozy Kona resorts to crowd black sand beaches and gawk at volcanoes.

A lone jeep sped away from Hilo International Airport. Its driver was a young man in his mid-twenties. He was a fit, unassuming man; your standard overachieving "All American" boy from a privileged suburban family. His fading high reg buzz cut and the Army issued assault pack resting in his passenger seat gave him away.

He sat erect and stiff in the driver's seat of the brown Jeep wrangler, jittery and on edge. But he never took his eyes off the road save for the quick peak at his phone's GPS and the occasional nervous glance in his rearview mirror.

He soon left town and headed towards Saddle Road which bisected the Big Island: a solid two-hour drive from Hilo to Kona. The jeep began to groan as he began the steady climb up "the hill," the over six thousand feet elevation change from sea level to above the clouds.

As he closed in on his destination, the tropical paradise began to fade away and was soon replaced by the vast dry lava fields that dominates the middle of the Island. As the snowy peaks of Mauna Kea and Mauna Loa began to loom, a cold wind began to blow through the open cabin of the jeep. Even through it was February, the tropical heat was a welcomed perk of island life; a cold winter wind was not. A shiver spread across his body. He didn't seem to mind; he was focused on his task at hand. Besides, the chill that crept up his spine, into his very soul, wasn't a result of mountain air.

The jeep began to slow as he arrived at his destination.

It was just a rock. Just a rock, he repeated in his head.

He drove up to the gate of the Pohakuloa Training Area. If he could just keep it together a little longer, this nightmare would be over. He just had to convince the gate guard it was business as usual. As he drove up to the guard he pulled out his CAC card and smiled.

"I'm just here to do a recon of the area. My units coming in a few months for gunnery and I'm just making sure we are set for my battalion's staff ride tomorrow." He kept smiling, though he knew his eyes looked tired. The bored gate guard, an elderly civilian security officer (who could barely hide the fact that he could care less), rendered a mocking salute.

Our man sat there for a second, exhausted from sleepless nights, staring blankly at the guard before returning the salute. After several seconds he began to creep the jeep forward and through the gate.

He drove slowly, and cautiously through the cantonment area of PTA. The whole base was practically a ghost town. He had made sure to do his homework: there was only some aviation support battalion out here training. More importantly, as he had checked the range schedule, no one should be training where he knew he needed to go.

The military police were scarce, most likely they were parked somewhere; either on their phones or taking a nap.

Now he just hoped the civilian workers wouldn't notice the dusty jeep wrangler slipping onto the tank trail. Hopefully, they just assumed he was another soldier on a snack run for his friends out in the lava fields.

He pressed down on the gas now, his heart rate climbing with the rpms. He shook in anticipation and began to sweat despite the cold air at 6500'. He was almost done.

Before him lay the vast sea of black rock that made up the training area. Nestled between the imposing colossi of Mauna Loa and Mauna Kea, these fields were the sights of battles and history so ancient that they'd been practically forgotten.

Now much of this land had been repurposed into live fire ranges and maneuver areas for the US Army. The ancient soil absorbing artillery shells and bombs over decades became a sore subject amongst the locals who called the Hawaiian Islands home.

He pulled over at a small range complex and grabbed his assault pack. He opened it quickly and ensured his precious cargo was still contained within.

"I'm sorry. I thought it was just a rock. I didn't realize. It's just a rock," he pleaded out loud shaking his head in dismay as he stared at black object.

He picked it up and stared at this odd lava rock. It was the approximate size and shape of a baseball, but with the deep black of a night sky, and smooth like polished obsidian.

Its surface was dotted with large sparkling pieces of peridot, a beautiful green gemstone, and sky blue larimar; gemstones formed in the molten forge.

Then he glanced at himself in the rear-view mirror. It was a miracle he made it through the gate without causing suspicion. He looked like shit. His eyes were red, bags still forming beneath them. His clothes looked disheveled and now that he didn't have to pretend, he looked like a maniac. He hadn't slept in months. He had really pissed off the wrong person. But as luck would have it, he was on the path to get back on her good side.

He looked at the woman sitting in his backseat. A beautiful Hawaiian in flowing white robes...glaring patiently at Second Lieutenant Dan Brookins.

The guard at the gate never saw her, because why would he? She was for Dan's eyes only. His punishment for his transgression had made that obvious. The chanting and beating drums in his head began to beat and scream all the louder as he continued his journey up the slopes, towards the volcano of Mauna Loa.

PART II

Three months ago, Second Lieutenant Dan Brookins had come out to PTA with his battalion on one of the many routine deployments to the Big Island.

Crammed into a small auditorium with a hundred other soldiers, he had to go through the notorious one hour "don't do this" brief. So many rules, so many fucks to not give.

He sat bored as hell, daydreaming during the bland welcoming from the range control civilians of PTA. This was his first time to the area, and he was relatively new to Hawaii in general. A fresh second lieutenant out of Ranger School, he was lucky to have received a platoon leader position right away. Rather than suffer the common fate of slaving away in his unit's S3, he was eager to get to work leading an infantry platoon. He could care less about the *nene* goose or whatever "sacred" areas were out here.

At the end of the brief, they were released from the auditorium to the smoke pits, gym, or queuing up to strip the small post shoppette bare of energy drinks and candy. As Dan took his place at the end of the gaggle, trying to squeeze through the exit, a range control civilian stood next to the doorway.

He was an old Hawaiian man with a long white beard, crooked smile, Pit Vipers, and a gut made probably by the hearty cooking of his wife. He smiled at Dan; the last one to the door.

When Dan reached him, they were the only two in the auditorium. The old local spoke with gentle reassurance, "First time on Big Island, LT? Just remember, don't take *the* lava rocks off this island."

Dan looked puzzling at him. "What do you mean *the* lava rocks?"

The Hawaiian chuckled, "LT, you may think this is just an open nothingness of wasteland. Most of you do. But this land... it doesn't belong to you. Shit, it doesn't even belong to *Na Kanaka.*"

He lowered his glasses with his chubby finger. His eyes hardened. He leaned in and Dan leaned back. Dan could smell cigarettes on his breath.

The man spoke softly. "Don't take the rocks. Stay out of the lava tubes. Be respectful out here, this is an ancient place. Ancient *and* very much aware you are not one of us. Nothing good is going to happen to you if you decide not to listen. Tell your men, too. There's been plenty of people who found this out the hard way."

Dan eventually broke into a nervous smile, "Sounds like a lot of trouble over a stupid rock."

"They aren't just rocks. Those rocks were once lava and magma, spewed forth by the volcanoes of this island. Created by the goddess *Pele.*"

"Okay..."

"This is *her* land, this island and everything on it still belongs to her." The man ushered Dan out the door, adding, "Don't forget."

As he walked out of the auditorium, Dan couldn't help but scoff. But when he turned around to glance one last time at the man, he was gone.

What a weird fucking guy, Dan thought to himself.

PART III

Two weeks later, Dan was under the stars nearing the conclusion of his unit's live fires. They'd spent the last two weeks maneuvering across jagged lava and generally being miserable. He was exhausted and ready to go home.

His company had bivouacked on what was known as "Range 20," a sprawling live fire area full of targets and mock objectives for the infantry to seize under the watching gaze of Mauna Loa. His command had decided to grant some mercy, letting the soldiers sleep through the night in the "non-tactical" comfort of a few heated tents.

Having finished a meeting with his platoon sergeant and squad leaders before bed down, Dan decided to get away and try to get some cell phone reception to text his girlfriend.

He looked up into the night and saw the Milky Way was out in full force. Until now he never appreciated how little light pollution there was out here. Without the full moon, he probably wouldn't have been able to see his own hands in front of him. Luckily, the moonlight helped guide him as he walked up the flattened path away from the sleeping tents towards and outcropping of lava rocks.

He found a flat rock to sit on before he looked around.

He was all alone. He took out his phone and opened his messages. Nina was back in Oahu. They had just moved in together and things were starting to get serious. He was glad to be texting her back and forth now that he had some time (and reception).

Dan: I should be home in a few days' babe.

Nina: Ok, I miss you. Can't wait to see you again. I'm still jealous you got to go to the Big Island. Think you'll be able to bring me home a souvenir?

Dan: Idk babe. We are pretty much locked down here and it's the middle of nowhere. Probably not in all honesty.

Nina: :(ok

Dan: But maybe I can find something cool from you, I'll try.

Nina: :) ok, I love you <3

Dan: <3 <3

Shit, he thought as he looked up.

Now he had to figure something out. He looked around. Nothing but fucking rocks. But then something caught his eye. It was a mass that stood out among the black. It was the opening to a lava tube, hidden by the jagged waves of the solidified lava.

He got an idea.

He got up and moved towards the opening of the lava tube. He stood at the edge and took out his flashlight. He squatted down and activated the white light, revealing a steep descent into the maw of the tube. It looked like it leveled out on the bottom. With little thought, he decided he was going on an adventure.

Before he could step off, Dan got the sensation he was being watched. He shut his light off and turned around. He scanned about him, maybe it was one of his soldiers? Range Control?

He heard movement to his left. Turning he saw a lone soldier sitting on a rock, staring at him. Though only several feet away, in this dark Dan couldn't tell who it was. The smell of smoke drifted into his nostrils, as the bright red cherry of a menthol cigarette lit up.

"You don't want that smoke, sir." Sergeant First Class Guerro, Dan's platoon sergeant, spoke plainly.

SFC Guerro sat staring off at the stars. He was on his last pump before he could drop his retirement packet. He was a twenty-year veteran with more deployments than any man Brookins knew. He'd been there, done that, and been around the block more than a few times.

"Trust me *LT*, you don't want that smoke." Guerro said again, this time with a little more salt in his voice.

"What are you talking about, *sergeant*?" Dan fired back as he stood. Despite his admiration for the man's experience, Dan and Guerro shared a mutual disdain for one another, each tolerating the other for the sake of getting the job done.

"You know it's bad luck to go in these lava tubes, just like it's bad luck to take rocks off the Island."

Dan scoffed, "That's just some bullshit superstition. I don't buy it."

SFC Guerro finished his cigarette and stomped it out. He sighed before saying flatly, "You ever stop to think that superstition exists for a reason?"

Even in the dark, the second lieutenant could feel Guerro's eyes on him.

Dan stared back, unsure what to say next. He didn't like to be challenged, but then again, Guerro's words had a way of sticking with him.

The two men sized each other up. SFC Guerro started to step away. "Whatever you do, don't let the joes fucking see you doing it, *LT*." He walked back towards the sleeping tents just as a cold wind began to blow.

Dan watched him leave before he turned back towards the mouth of the tube. He turned on his light and started his climb down the dark tunnel.

PART IV

Dan slid carefully slid down the steep face. Loose volcanic rock fell in a cascade towards the bottom. Other than these rocks and dirt, the tube was silent, making each movement sound like a thunder as he moved further into the abyss.

Dan finally reached the bottom and there he stood up. He was sure that he was the only living thing down here. He couldn't hear anything save for his own breathing.

He shined the flashlight around. The lava tube had at one point transported enormous quantities of spewed molten rock. It looked like it had been formed almost by modern drills, the walls were perfectly smooth. The tunnel looked like it went on for a long while, maybe to the heart of Mauna Loa itself.

Dan started walking, the floor being relatively smooth; dotted with small boulders that he had to weave between. His boot steps echoed loudly in the chamber in a steady beat.

But as he walked, something caught his attention. Either he was imagining things, or there was a delay with those echoes. As he walked he counted each step. There seemed to be a third step after his second.

He stopped and heard a small shuffle some place behind him. He resumed walking and listened intently; there it was!

It sounded like someone was trying to keep in step with him. He picked up his pace and then abruptly stopped. He heard it. A stutter step!

Dan whipped around and shined his light into the darkness behind him. He scanned back and forth, illuminating the abyss. Nothing besides rocks and darkness.

Something caught his eye. He illuminated a section of the tube to his right and walked forward. There were strange drawings and pictures carved into the walls.

Pale lines stood out brightly in the obsidian. Scenes of ways of life, of a long forgotten time, adorned the rock. He took out his phone and snapped a few pictures—this would make a cool story back home. He kept walking, shining his light left and right, gazing at the scenes depicted by the ancient Hawaiians.

All of a sudden, the tunnel came to an apparent end. Dan shined his light; it wasn't a cave in but instead layers of cooled lava piled together, like a wave frozen right before it's hellish break, one of those breaks that pulls a human down, down into treacherous depths. This must be the remains of the last lava flow to come through this tunnel, frozen obelisk of jagged lava rock spewed forth from the frozen wave; some were as big as Dan. But what caught his eye most was how the lava formed at the center of the tunnel.

The cooled lava had parted in the middle of the cave, forming a platform. Dan thought it almost looked like a seat; a throne fit for some denizen of the underworld. In the middle, and object was there. A stone. Dan walked forward.

He bent down and placed his hands on the stone. Maybe it was his imagination, but the stone seemed to hum and vibrate at his touch. As he picked it up, he felt the slightest of tugs, like there was a tether keeping it on its pumice throne.

That feeling relented as Dan pulled the stone closer.

He held it in one hand and shined his light. It was a rock, but a strange one.

The stone was a perfect sphere. It was the same size and dimensions of a baseball, a deep black like the night sky, and smooth like a polished piece of obsidian rock. It was light and felt like a cloud in his hand, but it was unquestionably solid. It sparkled with embedded gemstones, some as big as the nail on his thumb.

Nina would love this; she could use this for some artsy bullshit around the apartment.

Solution found. He smiled.

PART V

Dan unraveled the dump pouch on his belt; finally having a use for it. He placed the stone in the dangling piece of fabric before turning around and heading back where he'd come from.

As he walked away, he heard something behind him once again. Half a scoff, half a sob; like an angry woman in shock.

He shined his light towards the obelisks and the pumice throne behind him. The boulders and stones cast shadowy figures standing now in front of him. Dan felt he was in a crowded room all of a sudden with all eyes on him, but he was still sure he was all alone in this underground bowel of Mauna Loa.

It's just my imagination, he affirmed, and more than once.

He did a final sweep to satisfy his growing nervousness. Dan froze as his light passed over one of the man-sized stones. He could have sworn he'd seen a face peeking out from behind it. The face of a woman.

Imagination or not, he decided it was time to leave. He started airborne shuffling, moving briskly but watching his step as he moved towards the mouth of the tube.

As he walked out, he could have sworn he heard the soft beats of a drum and once again he couldn't doubt any longer that he heard footsteps almost matching his.

Dan picked up his pace, and suddenly stopped. Once again he heard that stutter step. He couldn't ignore the shred of doubt which now blared like and alarm in his head. *He wasn't alone.*

He took off sprinting, scrambling on all fours up the rock into the moonlight. At the top of the tunnel, he turned and shined his light…nothing.

Dan let out a sigh of relief: it was all in his head. But then he noticed something, something he must have missed. There were three strange piles of rocks now at the entrance to the lava tube: three towers of rocks stacked deliberately, and carefully on top of each other. *Were these always here? How did I not notice them before?*

Dan shook his head. He had to be imagining things and laughed out loud as he patted the dangling rock in his dump pouch.

But then he frowned. He heard a voice in his head: *"Don't take the lava rocks off this island. They don't belong to you."* Then the voice of his platoon sergeant, *"You ever stop to think that superstition exists for a reason?"*

Holding the strange, beautiful stone in his hands, Dan shook away these thoughts. He smirked, and he said aloud to no one in particular, "It's just a fucking rock."

PART VI

His troubles started subtly. Once he got home, Dan seemed to be on the wrong side of luck. Once his unit got back to Schofield Barracks, he embarrassingly couldn't seem to get his weapon clean at the armory. After several attempts, he couldn't get rid of the volcanic dust that seemed to pick up and move every time he cleaned his M4. After giving him a seemingly endless helping of shit, the armorers granted him mercy and finally accepted his weapon.

After enduring this embarrassment and tying up loose ends at the company area, he finally crawled to his car with his gear. However, he found that his car wouldn't start once he left his unit to go home. Once he got a jump and hit the road, he realized in the middle of the H1 traffic that his wallet was missing. Once he got back to his unit and tore apart his office, he found his wallet inexplicably on the passenger seat of his tan Toyota Tacoma. Then as his car passed the main gate, it died again in the middle of the intersection of Kunia road.

He finally got home past midnight and Nina was already asleep. When he finally laid his head down, he couldn't get the strange tune of tribal drums and chanting out of his head.

Must have been something I heard on the radio on the way home, he thought.

Eventually, he did go to sleep. That night he dreamt of a woman. Not Nina, or any woman he had ever met. She was a beautiful Hawaiian in flowing white robes. She stood before him on a field of molten lava, holding his gaze with a look that combined absolute rage, sadness, and undeniable beauty. The heat was excruciating and Dan cowered in pain. He awoke sweating with tears running down his face.

Discounting it as nothing more than a strange, lucid nightmare, he tried to go back to sleep. But the sound of drums and chanting was like a steady stream of driping water without end or an annoying song you couldn't shake from your head no matter how hard you tried.

The next morning, he woke up feeling like crap, but at least Nina was excited to see him again and that cheered him up.

They sat together drinking coffee as he told her his Big Island "war stories." He decided to leave out his adventure in the lava tube.

"Oh, I almost forgot!" he remembered suddenly. "I got you something, you said you wanted a souvenir." He fished out the lava rock and handed it to Nina. "I know it's just a rock, but you got to give me credit, I didn't have many options in that wasteland!"

She took it in her hands, examining it. "It's not just a rock," she laughed excitedly. "Do you see these green crystals?" She pointed to the sparkling stones within the rock. "These are peridot and olivine. And these blue crystals. Larimar."

Ever the expert, Dan smiled back at her as she continued, "They are native to Hawaii. They are made in lava, and very powerful in energy." Nina inspected the rock with even more scrutiny, "It's definitely an interesting stone. That's for sure."

She walked over to a small table where her crystal collection shared space with their fish tank. She placed the stone next to several others: Nina's "powerful" spiritual collection. As if on que, the small volcano in the fish tank spewed out a stream of bubbles.

"There," she said, giving him a sly smile. "*Now* the rock has a home." She gestured a *come hither* as she walked back into their bedroom.

Dan thought, *Maybe my luck's changing after all.*

PART VII

Three months later, Dan was sitting on the Hawaiian Airlines flight back to the Big Island, reflecting on how awful things had gotten.

First, it started with those fucking drums. It was something he'd heard at a luau he had once taken Nina to. But unlike a song stuck in his head, he couldn't shake it—ever. Every time he laid his head down, those drums beat and thundered back to horrid life.

A good night's sleep had become entirely foreign. Dan tried everything: pills, yoga, alcohol, meditating. Nothing worked. If he was lucky, exhaustion took him for a few hours. But the lack of sleep was taking its toll; he could feel his body and mind fracturing day by day.

In those times when he did manage, even then he wasn't spared. He would dream: the same dream, over and over again.

He would find himself alone among the lava fields of PTA, unsure of how he got there. It would always be night and preternaturally dark. Only the stars and the moonlight were there to guide him. He would wander for some time, lost.

Then he would hear them, the drums. Just like what

plagued him in waking life. But at first they would sound so far away. Soon they would grow louder, sounding nearer, and Dan could see small lights then in the distance. Like a snake of fire meandering through the lava rocks, there were torches.

As the drums got closer, so did the torches. Dozens of Hawaiian warriors, in full regalia, marching single file towards him. Some played the drums, others didn't. And they were getting closer, closer to Dan.

As they crossed in front of him, they all glared. Their anger was palatable, as if his gaze upon them was a heinous crime. Dan's eyes locked on the leader: an imposing man who wore the ornate cloak royalty, made of gold and crimson feathers of a thousand song birds. Behind him were several bodies carried on litters, each carried by several warriors. This was a funeral procession. As Dan's eyes met with this leader of the group, he felt the overwhelming compulsion to join them.

And so he did. A warrior angrily shoved a torch into his hand, and Dan took his place in the rear of the procession. One of them now, cross the lava fields and over rocks he walked for what seemed like eternity. Until finally they arrived to a massive hole in the ground. A lava tube.

As Dan watched, the warriors bearing the bodies descended into the dark cave. The procession continued, a steady pace downward to destinations unknown. Try as Dan could, he wasn't in control. His feet moved forward against his will and he struggled to avoid marching into the oblivion. But onward the procession marched, as the beating of the drums got louder and their torches dimmer. Into the darkness of the abyss, they marched. Into the belly of a dormant beast, they willfully marched. Until darkness was replaced by a dull orange glow. The procession was soon walking into a burning, flowing river. Dan was right there with them, even as they all swallowed by the fury of molten rock.

Dan always woke paralyzed. His eyes opened but he could not see, like he was blinded by some unknown force. A gasp stifled, too. He felt as if someone was sitting on his chest with hands wrapped around his throat; his lungs screaming out for air. As panic wracked his body, he would feel those hands curling tight on his throat, and how they'd begin to burn. Unable to resist his assailant's grip, Dan experienced a great heat; skin and meat charring to black; a heat so consuming he felt chills as nerves were burned away.

Just when he felt he would roast into a cloud of dust, he felt the hands leave him. With them, the awful heat so retreated. Sweat pooled all over his body as the pressure on his chest departed. Like some twisted perfume, as air flew desperately into his lungs he would smell the scent of sulfur, and how it floated away.

PART VIII

Nothing went his way. Things broke. His stuff went missing. Dan became a beacon of negative energy, his friendships evaporating for reasons he didn't expec tor understand. Weather rolled in to ruin new plans. The bank account was getting drained from unforeseen bills. Car stolen. A wayward stone rolling down a cliff had smashed his motorcycle and almost threw him into the sea.

Then there was Nina. He didn't even know how; he was still at a loss. They had their minor disagreements, but after four years of dating and moving out together to Hawaii; he had hoped they were finally getting serious.

But the couple started arguing, over the most random things. She seemed on edge around him and he seemed always on edge around her. Like there was this invisible force driving them apart but he didn't know what.

He tried to work things out, but to no avail. Things fell apart quick, and arguing turned to yelling, turned to fighting, turned to Nina moving out and then ghosting him. He had no idea where she went, but he didn't think she was coming back.

He cried every night, and when he did he couldn't even say for sure if it was over her or over his beyond-tortured insomnia.

PART IX

Before he went to PTA, Dan had been the Battalion rock star. The promising lieutenant being groomed to succeed in the Army, now was at the bottom of the barrel. A pariah in his own right.

Not only was he falling behind in training and his administrative actions, but he was suddenly falling out of favor with seemingly everyone. His platoon began to have issues, too: missing equipment, soldiers in trouble, stats falling, discipline ripping apart. Dan found that the interpersonal relationships he'd built had evaporated. His commander looked at him with disdain as his platoon had taken its place as the battalion's "problem children." His position as platoon leader was in danger and he could feel it. He tried and tried but he couldn't seem to make it back on track. The only track he was on was the track to become the battalion fuck up.

Things finally fell apart when during a squad live fire. Dan's M4 went off in his hands.

It—he—it, it sprayed an entire magazine, right in the middle of his platoon as the battalion commander watched.

No one died, other than Dan's career.

After an ass chewing that left him physically chafing, Dan was removed from his platoon that night and thrown down as an assistant to the assistant S4. Battalion fuck up had officially arrived.

He was staring at letter of reprimand from the commanding general. Everyone talked about how the "fucking LT" negligently discharged his weapon and almost wiped out a squad.

What they didn't know, and what Dan wouldn't dare say, was that he hadn't pulled the trigger. He couldn't say that he felt the bolt lock back and forward, sending rounds home to fire. He dared not share that he felt the selector switch move on its own from SAFE to AUTO.

As much as he wanted to scream to anyone who might listen, as much as he wanted to plead that it wasn't his fault...he couldn't say that something took control of his body, guiding him against his will, making him point his rifle towards the backs of his maneuvering platoon. On a beautiful Hawaiian day, he couldn't say that to his horror, the trigger had pulled back on its own.

PART X

There were a lot of things Dan couldn't say. Any utterance of the unlucky and unfortunate events that now plagued his life would mean the end of him—not just in the Army but for the rest of his life! He would be labeled a maniac. A nutjob. Insane. Like a veil lifted from his eyes, something truly strange was happening. In addition to his stream of atrociously bad luck, there seemed to be something otherworldly at play.

On a particularly strange night on the jungle land navigation course, he began to notice things. Things hiding between the leaves, darting out of sight before he could get a good look. That night, Dan saw things, things in the bushes that were throwing rocks at him. He finally had enough and turned on his light. What he did find were little footprints in the mud.

Small, little bare feet.

Hoping it was a local kid who snuck onto the training area, when he saw a shadow behind a tree he chased a figure through the elephant grass. He cornered it between a rock and a ravine and flashed his headlamp's red lens. Whatever it was, it went giggling as it crashed through thick grass. Dan decided it wasn't worth getting into an altercation with some punk kid. He turned around and continued trying to find his navigation points in the dark.

Dan thought he was on the right track, but when he finally found a point he was frustrated to find that it wasn't the navigation point he needed. He dotted over his map with a red lens; confused as to where he was.

As he crouched there in the dark, he heard a little voice, "Well, it's obviously not here. Have you tried walking a little more to the north?"

Dan froze. The voice sounded like it was right next to

him. He turned his head, slowly, until the red light of his headlamp came to rest on the spot where he'd heard the voice. His eyes grew wide.

What he saw looked like little Hawaiian woman sitting on a small log with and smug smile on her face. The longer he stared the more the hairs on the back of his neck stood up. He noticed that while she looked human, under the red light her features looked…off. That and she was the size of a toddler. Dan stared, wide-eyed and in shock. He rubbed his eyes and prayed he was just imagining things.

In the hue of red, he could see that her eyes reflected the light. She raised an eyebrow.

Dan's light began to spontaneously blink and then faded out completely. In the darkness once more, he could see that her eyes glowed blue now, and he suddenly heard: "What did you say about superstitions before?"

Before Dan could act, she dove into the darkness.

Fuck this, he thought, and he took off running. Heart pounding against his chest, he just wanted to get out of the jungle.

Of course, when he returned, he learned he was the last one done and hadn't found any of the correct points. The other soldiers snickered, but he didn't care. He just wanted to go home. He just wanted to get away from this jungle.

But after that night, Dan started to notice other things. Strange things out of place, whispers—movements out of the corner of his eye. He would look up and see beady, glowing orbs, peering out of dark corners as he passed. Not animal eyes, but something more human, glances of what looked like little people moving behind cover.

Those things messed with him. They taunted him. They stole his belongings and broke his things from the shadows and behind his back. He hated being alone because they took full opportunity to torment him. Whatever or whoever they were.

Sometimes, as he laid in bed struggling to sleep, something would tug at his toes. He would bolt up and hear something run away into the darkness of his apartment. But even if Dan couldn't see them, he would hear the fleeing pitter patter on the floor, and what sounded like giggling after, behind the walls.

And when he thought his apartment was quiet and still, a whisper would come from nowhere. That same taunt he'd heard in the jungle: "What did you say about superstitions before?"

PART XI

Dan began to notice a white mongrel mutt. He saw this fucking dog everywhere. Sitting on a corner, outside his window, watching from afar, up close, even running alongside his car has he raced down the highway. The dog followed him everywhere.

Sometimes it would run up and snarl, bluff charging him when he least expected it. Other times it would watch him from afar.

Even his apartment didn't offer him shelter from this strange dog. He could hear its tell-tale pacing outside his door. With the occasional low whine, an annoying scratch would claw against the wood. But every time when Dan would throw open the door, ready to kick the dog away: no dog. But there were white hairs on the floor.

But the oddest quirk was that only Dan could see it. When he attempted to point it out to others, he would receive all manners of puzzled looks.

Then the "warrior," or that's what Dan called him. He looked like a Hawaiian he had seen in all those paintings and pictures at the Bishop Museum when Nina would drag him there. Chiseled, ripped, dangerous looking.

As far as Dan could tell, he was the only one who could see him too. Just like the dog, when he would point the warrior out, he would receive the same looks and dismissals. People were beginning to question just how "all there" Dan was. Dan decided it was best to keep his mouth shut; permanently shut, shut about everything.

But not the warrior. He screamed and danced at Dan in the darkness. Challenging him, speaking some language Dan could only assume was ancient Hawaiian.

Dan would often times look up in horror to see the warrior swinging a traditional Hawaiian axe at his head. As Dan recoiled in fear, bracing for death, he would reopen his eyes to see the massive man standing over him. Glaring. Eyes filled with hate. This occurred several times a day. Usually, the warrior would be waiting in a dark room or just out of sight.

But luckily for Dan, the warrior was nothing more than an apparition. As much as a threat he seemed, he never followed through.

However, a mangy mutt, a ghostly warrior, nightmares, these weren't even close to being the worst.

The woman. A beautiful Hawaiian woman, unlike any woman he had ever seen. The one from his dreams. She appeared as if painted into life. She was tall and athletically built, like the many of the local surfers he had seen battling the waves on the North Shore of Oahu. Eyes deep blue like the ocean, hair a deep black like fresh hardened lava, and her skin was the color of a red and volcanic soil.

Like the many other sights that plagued Dan, he soon saw her everywhere. But unlike his other "visions," she kept her distance. Always at a distance.

And she was angry. Very angry. Hate, malice, sadness, all of these adorned her face. Those deep blue eyes bore a hole straight through his soul. Dan found eye contact was unbearable, he felt like a child every time he tried. Fear stirred in his belly as soon as her gaze fell upon him. Dan would keep his face down and desperately tried to escape her.

The woman kept her distance. But every time Dan saw her, she seemed to get closer with each sighting. Slowly closing in no matter how much he tried to avoid her. Like she was an inevitable conclusion. She terrified Dan the most.

Part XII

"I have to be going *insane*," Dan said to himself one early morning, sitting in the parking lot of the Base Exchange.

He started beating the steering wheel with his hands. A scream rose from his lungs as he lost his shit. That had to be the answer.

He had to have been going insane.

He had to have been unravelling. Imagining things that weren't there, taking images he had seen in this tropical shithole people call paradise and projecting into reality in some bizarre waking nightmare. He stopped beating the wheel as his voice became hoarse.

His life and career in shambles in three months. That was the only answer to this. It was all in his head and this was just some Hawaiian-themed nervous breakdown, psychotic episode.

Dan looked at his bloodshot eyes in the mirror. He was fucking exhausted. He needed coffee before he headed in to continue his slow rot behind a computer screen, picking away at redundant PowerPoints. He opened his car door, slowly, half expecting to hit some kid he hadn't noticed or have his door taken off by some freak parking lot accident. But luckily, for once, nothing happened.

Dan hurriedly walked into the exchange building to its corporate coffee shop. He got his acidic fast-food coffee and a chewy mass-produced bagel before heading back outside. He looked at his watch and noticed he had some time before he was expected to be at work. He decided to sit in the sun and find some semblance of relaxation. He found a bench where he could sit, be alone, because at least he could control that in his life. He sat down and stared at the ground as he chewed on his bagel.

"Mind if I take a seat, *LT*?" Before Dan could say anything a man sat down next to him.

Dan sighed. Dan didn't bother to look up until he smelled a menthol cigarette.

"Sergeant First Class Guerro, you're still here? I thought you'd retired?"

"Not yet, I'm starting my terminal leave tomorrow." He took a drag. "Just living the dream."

"Wish I could say the same," Dan said.

Guerro turned to him and offered him a stick. "You look

like you need one."

Dan never smoked before; he had always viewed it as beneath him.

"Fuck it," he said and grabbed the cigarette. Dan soon took a drag and stifled a cough, feeling the nicotine surge through him.

"So, what's up with you, LT? It's been a while." SFC Guerro looked at Dan quizzically. "Also, you look like shit." A flash of concern briefly came across his face.

Dan looked at that weathered face and then looked at the cigarette in his own hand. He weighed whether or not he should say anything.

"It's just a really weird time in my life, Guerro." Dan sighed as his throat started to tighten up.

Guerro just raised his brow at his former platoon leader. "Yeah? So, tell me about it."

And so Dan did, holding nothing back as he poured out his soul. Everything from the lava tube to Nina, the rock, his bad luck, the dreams, the visions, all the weird shit that tormented his life he laid before Guerro's feet.

SFC Guerro took a long drag after and looked at the sky. He blew out his smoke and threw his cigarette on the ground.

"You know that I'm half Hawaiian? On my mom's side. I lived on Oahu and Kauai almost my whole life before enlisting." Guerro paused and looked at Dan. "And, yeah, I believe you, Brookins, and I tried to warn you."

"What the fuck do you mean 'tried to warn me'?" Dan said, getting frustrated.

"I grew up with all the legends and stories, and to make a long story short, there are things here that shouldn't be fucked with. And *you* fucked with them."

Dan snorted and snidely remarked, "I told you I don't believe in that shit—"

"Well maybe you fucking should, Brookins. Like I said, superstition exists for a reason. *Especially* in Hawaii."

"So, what do you think? That I'm cursed or something?"

"Yes. You are cursed. You should have never gone down into that fucking lava tube, and you *definitely* shouldn't have taken that rock."

"Bullshit. No offense, it's all bullshit." Dan threw his own cigarette down.

Guerro looked into Dan's eyes, intense and grave. "It doesn't matter what you think, Brookins. This place? This island? It doesn't belong to us. There are things that dwell on these islands that aren't human. Some things that are borderline demonic. And should not be fucked with."

Dan held his gaze, a sheen of sweat forming under his brow. He was unable to find any words. His mind was on Guerro's.

Guerro stood up. "Look, I can't help you; only you can. Whether you believe me or not, you're cursed and there's only one way to fix your problem. You know what you have to do."

Dan watched as he walked away. Dan sat there for what felt like a long while, lost in thought. Eventually his phone began to vibrate; a sign he was late to work. He dumped his coffee and threw his bagel to a group of waiting chickens. Dan pushed out of his mind any thought of curses or whatever bullshit mumbo jumbo.

Part XIII

Later that night he sat in his empty, loveless, lonely apartment. Slumped in a lazy boy, he was tired and drunk. A cheap radio garbled a static-laced song. His second bottle of cheap liquor, three quarters gone, had spilled plenty over his shirt and onto the floor. Dan hoped that borderline poisoning would send him into some semblance of rest. He'd take any amount of sleep in exchange for a killer hangover. He was a shell of the man he'd been a mere three months prior.

He turned over and vomited onto the floor. *Cursed? What a load of shit.*

And yet a dog scratched at his door, a Hawaiian warrior glared from the corner of his living room, and small heads with shining eyes peered around the corner of his hallway.

"This is all just in my head," he slurred as he leaned back. "None of you are real!"

He stared blankly at the rock in the fish tank now. Nina had taken her collection of stones with her, but she'd unceremoniously dropped the rock in the fish tank when she left. The large black stone just sat there, like a glimmering black portal. Like a black hole sucking the life out of Dan.

Dan stood up from his chair and stumbled his way over. Splashing water about and startling the fish, he pulled out the stone and held it in his hands.

The same size and dimensions of a baseball, smooth and deep black like the night sky. A polished piece of obsidian rock sparkling with gemstones forged from lava.

The longer he stared, the more he felt his blood pressure rise. He held the stone tighter in his hands as his knuckles turned white and he started to shake.

"Fuck you! I'm not cursed! I'm not fucking cursed!" He screamed as he shook with frustration. "This is just a fucking rock. You're just a fuckin' rock!" He threw the rock against the wall. It impacted dead center a picture of Dan and Nina, shattering the glass. The stone fell to the floor with an indifferent thud.

Dan took a step forward and took a drunken stumble. The warrior vanished from the apartment with a grunt, the little people ran in fear, and the dog at his door gave a nervous whimper.

The radio began to blare static, until the unmistakable sound of tribal drums and chanting blasted from it and the sound consumed the room. It was so loud that Dan covered his ears as he lay in a pile on the floor. Then suddenly the room went silent, like a vacuum sucked of all noise. Dan uncovered his ears and unsteadily he rose.

He wiped the sweat off his face. It was getting hotter, and hotter. Dan was starting to sweat like he was in a sauna. He stumbled to the thermostat to turn on the air conditioning…it read 103F, and was climbing.

Dan turned to the fish and heard a bubbling, hissing noise. The little fish tank looked like it was boiling as the toy volcano was spewing forth a stream of bubbles. Suddenly the fish tank burst in a spectacular shattering of its own glass, and what looked like lava began to pool and flood his apartment from its remains.

Dan recoiled: his floor was actually becoming lava. He stumbled back away from the growing lake of fire until he tripped and fell forward. He landed into the searing heat, and he could feel his body blister and burn. He tried to stand, but his melted muscle and burned away nerves prevented such feats. He tried to scream but his lungs and vocal cords were properly scorched. He lay in agony as he burned on the twenty-eighth floor of a Honolulu apartment while his neighbors probably slept peacefully.

Before his eyes melted and his brain was fried, he was able to look up to see a looming figure.

That beautiful Hawaiian woman dressed in white robes

stood in the middle of the room, glaring; the fire, heat, lava, all radiating out from where she stood. She held the stone in her outstretched hand. He could feel her anger and although he was still burning alive, a cold chill ran down what was left of his spine.

Then her face changed: solemn, deepened sadness. Suddenly, she vanished: stone falling to the floor.

The radio began to play, sound returning to the room. Dan could hear downtown Honolulu from an open window. He was no longer burning; he didn't feel any more pain. In fact, he was fully intact, as a peculiar part of his mind knew he would be.

Dan looked around the room. He was finally alone. Besides the broken frame and glass on the floor, the room was untouched. For a moment he thought it was all just a intoxicated nightmare. That is until Dan looked up to see a shattered fish tank and several doomed goldfish frantically flopping around. Dan crawled forward to the rock, picking it up, cradling it in his hands.

The words echoed in his mind: *Don't take the lava rocks off this island. There's one way to fix your problem.*

Dan knew what he had to do.

PART XIV

As the imposing height of Mauna Loa loomed over him

beneath a fiery, fading sky, Dan snapped out of his daze. He checked his watch: 1754 27 November 2022.

He looked to his left to see the white dog trotting along. He pulled off the bumpy tank trail and onto an assembly area. Dan parked behind some dumpsters, out of sight, just in case someone may have questions about an abandoned jeep.

This was as far as he could go. The rest of the way was on foot.

He stepped out of his vehicle and walked over to his backseat, opening it as a gentlemen would for his lady. Though he couldn't see her at the moment, he knew she was there. He paused for a moment then shut his back door. He felt a sudden blast of heat as something brushed his cheek. Her hand, he suspected. That heat vanished when a mountain wind accosted him. He checked his bag and made sure the stone was still safely secured. Then he zipped it shut.

Dan turned around and looked at the white mongrel sitting patiently behind him. "I guess it's just you and me now," he said.

Dan stepped off towards their final destination, and the dog began to trot at his side. The drums and chanting began to beat as he climbed up the slope.

As the fading sun set the sky on fire, the old Hawaiian's voice echoed in his head, the first of many ignored warnings:

"Don't take the lava rocks off this island."

He paused to catch his breath, the elevation here was over 6500 feet. His lungs could feel it as his heart beat heavily in his chest. It was also much colder at this elevation at sunset. Every breath he took sent a cloud from his mouth into the air. Dan shivered beneath his meager "winter" clothing. Before he continued, he looked around. The landscape was covered in the black and grey blanket of cooled lava. To the unknowing, this place was nothing more than a wasteland. But not Dan. He knew better now.

The sky was getting dark, and Dan was starting to get nervous about having to find his way. But soon he scrambled up the slopes to the familiar maw of a tube.

The warrior stood before him at the mouth of the lava tube, arms crossed and scowling. Waiting patiently for the deed to be done. Out of the corner of his eye, Dan spied glowing orbs peering over the boulders; little figures darting out of sight before he could look.

This was the place.

He stood before the hole in the ground and couldn't help but reflect on that fateful decision three months ago. He stood frozen, thinking. A bark snapped him out it and he saw the white cur run into the darkness of the tube.

"It's now or never," Dan heard himself say.

The beating of the drums was almost ear splitting as he descended. He dug a flashlight out of his pack and shined its light into the darkness.

He hurriedly paced the length of the tube until he came upon a familiar sight: the obelisk of black stone and a frozen deluge of hardened lava.

The white dog came up behind him, nudging him along with a wet nose as he nervously stepped towards the throne formed in the center of the cave.

As Dan approached, he suddenly sank to his knees in exhaustion, his self-inflicted burden was almost done.

Dan took off his pack and fished out the stone. He inched closer as his hands began to shake, and he held his breath as he returned it to its welcoming home.

As it began to touch the volcanic rock, Dan could feel the slightest tug.

He could feel the concussions of the drums now; the chanting overwhelming. Tears flowed from his eyes.

Dan no longer held the stone.

Silence. The drums had stopped, the chanters had gone. Dan remained, sunken to his knees, surrounded by silence and the flashlight he hadn't even known he'd dropped.

He felt a rumbling in the earth, like a wave on the ocean had passed underneath him. The walls of the tube shook and debris started to from the ceiling. Dan turned around, grabbing his flashlight and shining it on the white dog who was still with him. It was whining. Dan decided that he wasn't ready for this place to be his tomb. He began moving back the way he'd came.

The dog ran ahead of Dan, and in the darkness the ground continued to shake. Dan scrambled up and out of the tube, resting on his knees at the top. He stared into the now dark, black sky. It was much colder now; he could feel it in his bones as the wind cut through him, causing a spasm of shivers.

The ground shook violently as the sound of cracking earth exploded forth, and a red glow appeared at the top of Mauna Loa. Dan looked in horror as lava spewed from fissure vents and volcanic ash was sent into the sky. The night was chased away by the awesome glow of nature's fury.

The dog trotted beyond Dan and sat beside the feet of the woman. A Hawaiian woman in flowing white robes; imposing, beautiful and radiant. She was the power beneath Dan. She was the rage beneath the earth.

"Pele," escaped from his mouth, and he whispered it softly. His eyes filled with wonder and fear.

She smiled. Now, he understood.

The stone was part of her. Just like this entire island was nothing more than a part of her. Part of her anger and joy flung from the deepest part of the earth. Which now had awakened once more as it raged, creating new land as it destroyed the old. Her destruction and creation. Each piece of stone was a reminder of her, part of her. But the odd stone he'd snatched from beneath the earth *was* her.

Dan returned the smile as his face was lit by the glowing of lava now flowing like a river down the slopes. She walked towards him, once again placing a hand on his cheek as she looked into his eyes. She turned and observed her work, a white dog by her side.

Dan slowly laid down, embracing the forgiving forces beneath him, and closed his eyes. The ground was warm and he no longer felt the cut of the cold mountain air. The volcano didn't worry him, nothing did. Not anymore. He welcomed the deep, comforting sleep that came next. In its embrace, beneath an ancient sky on sacred ground, he dreamt of lava and raging gods.

"Pele's curse can last for days, months, and even years after picking the lava rocks. It's believed that the only way to rid yourself of the curse is to return the "stolen" item to the island. This explains why numerous tourists write letters to the [Hawaii Volcano] National Park begging the rangers to return the rocks on their behalf"

—*Hawaii Guide*

A FEAST UNSEEN IN AGES

PART I

In the cradle of civilization, a city burned.

Gunfire and explosions echoed through the night, a perfect camouflage of chaos and madness in a city that had turned itself into a veritable inferno. It was the end of day two, and the Second Battle of Fallujah burned. Tracer fire lashed out at coalition aircraft overhead, resulting in rocket and cannon fire that silenced the source permanently. Precision bombs were dropped from high flyers, impacting onto the foreheads of the unlucky insurgents below. Somewhere in the distance the distinctive "thump-thump-thump" of a 40mm cannon raining down from the heavens above, revealed that an AC-130 "Spooky Gunship" swung its scythe over the Fallujah night.

Such a field of death ready for harvest. Shouts of men in combat echoed across the urban sprawl, the ghostly wails of the dying and suffering competed with the sounds of abject violence. Dark shadows with malign intent crawled just out of sight. All the while, foreign fighters with a death wish lay patiently in snipers' nests, and local boys prowled the alleyways and rooftops with RPGs at the ready. The civilians who hadn't fled the city desperately huddled together; praying to make it through the night while bombs fell and dark shadows scratched at their doors.

Cpl Martinez and the marines of Third Platoon were part of the effort to put the fire out. It was the battle for Fallujah, *the second one*, and the task would be daunting.

Operation Phantom Fury had been launched to secure the Iraqi city, which had been overran by insurgent forces led by Abu Musab al-Zarqawi. The drums of war had been beaten in the city for weeks, and the extremist sects had succeeded in staging a full on uprising. Foreign fighters had flooded the city from all corners of the Islamic world; some five thousand of them had spent the last several months turning Fallujah into a veritable fortress. The insurgents knew the Americans couldn't allow them to hold such influence (especially before the Iraqi elections) and had been making the preparations to welcome them. Tunnels had been dug, buildings turned into death traps, ambushes set, and thousands upon thousands of weapons and even more ammunition had made it into the city. If the Americans wanted to take it, the followers of al-Zarqawi would make them bleed for it.

It was night two of the battle, and it was far from over. The Coalition forces were taking the city street by street, house by house, and room by room. A machine gun nest or a child's nursey sat just behind the corner. It was tedious as it was deadly. Fallujah had quickly become the most dangerous place on earth. The horror of uncertainty and the unknown ran rampant for the men and women tasked to walk gun's up and liberate.

For all the technological advances that the Western armies had, men like Cpl Martinez needed to get their hands dirty to root out the enemy. Insurgents could literally be anywhere, anyplace, waiting to blast men like Martinez in the face when he least expected it.

Third Platoon had been tasked this night to do what they did best: kill. Conducting what was known as "search and destroy," their task was to push past the current line of troops and kill, or destroy anything of use to the enemy. That meant looking for staging areas for the insurgent forces, weapon caches, and any command-and-control nodes. It was a grunt's dream, a genuine, free-fire search and destroy. It was the Wild West.

There were threats that the marines needed to find. Enemy mortar teams had been peppering Coalition forces and MANPAD teams laid in weight to shoot down any medevac chopper they could get the drop on. These enemy used the terrain to their advantage, firing and slipping away into the maze of buildings before counterfires could wipe them out. These threats needed to be dealt with the old-fashioned way: Cpl Martinez and the marines of Third Squad were on the hunt.

Martinez and his platoon rounded a corner, and shots immediately rang out. Across the street, a machine gun opened up from what appeared in the darkness to be a small building. Additional muzzle flashes from AK-47s then erupted; probably from its windows. The distinctive noise of a venerable RPG shrieked into the fray, and the rocket propelled grenade sailed towards them.

An ambush. A sloppy one.

These insurgents were determined, but luckily for the marines, this group was not some of the battled hardened fighters from the likes of Chechnya and Al Qaeda. They were just young, but fanatical men who answered the holy call to kill the infidel invaders.

The machine gunner fired too early. His long burst aimed at Martinez's point man went high, sending tracers over the point man's head while he dived for cover. Tracers lit up the dark street in bursts of green death. Then a loud "clack!" sounded as that dirty weapon jammed.

The others inside the building fired and fired. Like their man on the machine gun, they probably only had the faintest idea of how to use their weapons. Everything in the night air was struck but the marines. The RPG gunner fired at them, impacting against the corner the marines were rounding, sending rubble everywhere but having no other effect. Unlike the Americans, these attackers lacked night vision. They used flashlights to try and illuminate the marines. Hopped up on drugs and fanaticism, these fighters may have botched their ambush, but they were still dangerous and looking to win at any cost. As the Americans spread out, the insurgents redoubled their fire.

However, unlike the insurgents, the men of Third Platoon were beyond lethal.

The marines remembered the training that had been drilled into them, repetitions beyond count. Hand signals and shouts communicated, the marines took cover and set up a base of fire. Their M16s barked in three round bursts and gunners fed their M249s; sending a hail of 5.56 towards the insurgents.

Two marines let loose with their M203s; sending 40mm grenades into windows where they exploded in a flash.

At this point, Martinez would have begun maneuvers to close with and kill the insurgents.

But just like that, the battle was over. The enemy fire just stopped. Like a switch had been flipped, the gunfire was simply gone.

A cease fire was called, and the marines began to cautiously move toward the enemy position. In the green light of their night vision, they saw they were approaching what had once been a restaurant.

PART II

It was possible that the marines had killed them all, but the gunfire falling that sudden? Martinez and his men had all been briefed that their foe was made up of diehards willing to fight until the bitter end. The more seasoned marines' hackles instantly went up, their foe was also not afraid to play dead. This could well be a tactic to draw them into yet another ambush.

Trap or not, the order was called to clear the building. First Squad moved in on the restaurant. Cpl Martinez bounded with his team with his finger on the trigger and eyes weary for movement. It was impossible to know what the enemy would do next. The marines also had to be aware that there were civilians still in the city. A shadow behind a window could easily be a child or a curious grandfather.

Slow is smooth, and smooth is fast, Martinez reminded himself. Getting sloppy could mean disaster for him or his marines.

Martinez and his team took cover behind a car that was in front of the restaurant. So far, the insurgents hadn't opened fire. Could mean they were dead, could mean they had run, or they could be playing possum. The marines had been briefed that insurgents were likely to play dead or wounded to get as close as possible to drop a grenade or pull a fast draw.

Martinez scanned the building with his NVGs. No movement. Besides the gunfire and explosions of the battle off in the distance, it was silent.

He scanned his sectors with his team...something caught his eye in the darkness. Beyond one of the large open-air windows of the restaurant, there was now move-ment. A shadow rose. It resembled a person for a split second, but it registered with Martinez that it seemed thin and lanky; it was too dark to get much more detail. Maybe it was one of the insurgents ready to get the fight underway again? Cpl Martinez stared through the hazy green of his NVGs and the shadow seemed to turn its head to then stare in his direction. Martinez felt his hair stand on end.

The figure was staring *at* him, through the darkness, and he somehow knew it. Worse yet, the figure's eyes glowed bright, like a predator's eyeshine. Before he could even consider squeezing his trigger, who— or *what*ever it was, turned and moved out of site. Despite the humid night air, Cpl Martinez felt a chill surge through his body.

He suddenly felt as if he saw something he shouldn't have.

"What the fuck was that?" He heard himself say.

"What was what, Corporal?" whispered Lance Corporal Barnes, still staring down the barrel of his M16.

Cpl Martinez snapped himself out of it, replying, "Thought I saw movement at my twelve-o clock. Could be one of the gunmen. Get your rifle on that window." The figure seemed nowhere in sight. He had to get focused again, any distraction could mean life or death.

Martinez's squad leader called Third Squad forward and they began to stack up on a side door. Martinez took his spot as the third man in the stack, eyeing the wall of the restaurant. Those insurgents may have gone quiet, but the marines needed to make sure that they were indeed dead.

The lead marine moved forward and with three blasts of a shotgun blasted off the door hinges, after delivering a kick that sent the door falling, back into the darkness of the restaurant. The marines then surged into the breach. They moved with deadly deliberateness; drill after drill had made them adapt at maneuvering the long eighteen-inch barrels of their M16s in confined quarters.

They moved quickly, sweeping room after room, corner after corner. A staircase revealed the entrance to a second story. Slowly, up the stairs the marines moved. No insurgents, but they found a nice sniper's nest and a cache of weapons.

But no enemy. No bodies. It was like they had all just vanished.

Cpl Martinez found signs that the firefight hadn't been in their heads. Before his boots lay a mess of blood and dirt and shell casings from an AK-47. No bodies, though. Weapons, yes; abandoned on the floor. Lots of blood, that too; on the ground, dark, warm, and sticky. The marines definitely had hit someone, but—

"Maybe they dragged him off?" another marine said to Martinez. "But where?"

The corporal looked around and it hit him—this was the spot he had seen that shadow. He suddenly got a bad feeling in the back of his head.

On the ground were a few prints, expected if someone dragged off a body. But in the blood, Martinez noticed the footprints were barefoot. Not too unusual, many Iraqis walked around without shoes. On the wall right then, dropping his stomach, something held his gaze.

It was a singular handprint. A bloody contour. And it was...wrong. It was much bigger than a man's; its thin fingers as long as Martinez's whole hand.

The other marines had stopped to stare at it too, all in silent bewilderment.

"Corporal," Barnes said, "check it out. A blood trail."

Down the hall towards another staircase was indeed a

trail of blood, the kind smeared onto a dirty floor by a dead body dragged by eager hands. Guns up, the marines followed. It led them down the stairs, towards a back door that hung ajar before opening into the unknown night.

The marines crept closer and stared out the doorway, following with their night vision the gleams of the blood trail. It seemed to paint its way into a meager alleyway and then onto a backstreet. Past some trashcans, the trail stretched a bit farther and at its end lay a body abandoned around a corner. The white robe "man jammies" and soviet style chest rig gave the body away as one of the insurgents. The marines could see the glazy gaze of death. The body's jaw and nose were missing, too, its neck a ruin. Whatever life it carried was gone now, just a still mess of flesh.

Suddenly the body jerked around the corner and out of sight. The marines raised their rifles and got behind what cover they could. The insurgents could just be around the corner; it was rare for them to recover the dead, which meant they could be planning to come back once the marines left.

As they waited, a face appeared around the corner. Under the green hue of their NVGs, details were not always clear. But this face was clear enough. Hauntingly so. It looked like a man crouched on all fours, peering around the corner. He looked like the shadow Martinez had seen; thin and gaunt. He, no, this was no man.

Under Martinez's green filter, its skin was still pale and sickly. Its head was humanlike, yes, but all wrong, like if a human's face was removed of all its hair and then stretched over a skull that was too large. Its mouth seemed cavernous, hanging open as it stared at the marines.

Martinez at first thought it was drooling. Liquid dripped from its sharp, pointed teeth...but Martinez squinted until he realized what he was looking at was blood. Its hands, wrapped around the corner of the alley, had caused that horrid print on the wall, but what stood out most was its eyes. Set deep in its face, large pits glowed in their center.

Cpl Martinez had taken fire, been caught in explosions, even taking a round to his flak. War had never made him feel like he did now. He wanted to run, faster than his racing heart. He was afraid.

This creature that peered out, around the corner and eyed the marines, it gave them the faintest smile, then it vanished around the corner.

The marines stood in stunned silence before one of them blurted out nervously, "Ugh, did anyone else see that weird fuckin' dog?"

"That wasn't a fucking dog, bro."

"Then what the fuck was that, dude?"

"I don't know, man. I don't know what the fuck that was," Cpl Martinez whispered.

Was it a man? Some fucked up animal? An escaped

monkey maybe? Martinez's mind began to wander. But Marines didn't long to sit around and ponder what they had just seen. All of them wanted to get the fuck away from this place. They still had a mission to do, too, freaks running around Fallujah or not.

The squad leader called out for the marines to rally back up together.

Third Squad rejoined the rest of the platoon and Martinez was called up with the other team leaders.

"Listen up," the squad leader said. "Command is calling for a change of mission. Scouts spotted some activity in what looked like some ruins on the outskirts of the city. Looked like mortar teams setting up, and two squad-sized elements. Oorah, Marines?"

Most of the marines growled out a sharp "Kill!" and "Get Some!" in institutionalized motivation. While others responded with a soft "Oorah." desperately trying to distract themselves from the borderline demonic event they had just witnessed.

"Rah," Martinez let out, rolling his eyes in the dark, thinking, *Whatever you say, Big Sarge.*

PART III

The marines were up and moving through the city. Between the sounds of war it was eerily quiet, save the jingle of equipment and their own bootsteps. This part of the city was a ghost town. No more ambushes challenged the marines, but Cpl Martinez couldn't help but feel that they were being watched.

Then at one point, if he didn't know any better, he kept seeing a figure running along the rooftops just almost out of sight. A slender figure, not unlike what he saw before, running on all fours and leaping across the gaps like some twisted mix of a dog and a monkey. As they barreled down the maze of Fallujah towards their objective, all the marines of Third Platoon caught a glimpse of that humanoid figure; peering at them from some corner and they felt a gnawing fear in their stomachs. They all were tired, war had taken its toll, surely it was all in their heads.

They came to a halt just outside their objective and cleared a two-story building. The marines quickly set up a well-defended patrol base, the last thing they needed was to let their guard down now. The night was still young and dangerous.

Martinez crouched just out of sight behind a window. He still peered cautiously at the rooftops, spying a pair of glowing eyes still peering down at the marines.

No one was shooting at them, no IEDs had gone off, no mortars had landed near them yet.

More dangerous things to worry about I guess, Martinez mused.

Whatever it was, it didn't seem like it was a threat and was keeping its distance.

For now, at least, he thought. As if drugged-out insurgents weren't bad enough. Now he had to worry about monsters in the dark.

"Yo, Corporal, check it out. Got movement across the street."

Cpl Martinez peered out from the window some one hundred yards down the street. An Iraqi man slowly crept across.

"I see him, I see one military-aged male. Any weapons?" Cpl Martinez asked.

"Looks wounded but I see an AK-47, should we smoke him?"

"No, let him pass. Let's not give away our location."

As Martinez watched the Iraqi, he saw that indeed he did clutch an AK, and that he walked with a noticeable limp. It was hard to tell if he was a civilian or an insurgent. Martinez had learned this conflict had a way of blurring the lines.

All of a sudden, the man began firing into the dark. The marines tensed up, holding their fire as they watched. The gunfire wasn't directed at them, but something behind the man.

The man fired wildly, until a blur blitzed across the street. The shadowy form seized the man, whose AK-47 went flying. The shadowy form had been joined by two others; who'd leapt from the roofs, down onto the street.

There are three of them.

The three figures had the struggling man, each grabbing a limb. The Iraqi screamed hysterically until each was rewarded with a different prize.

"Fuck this," a marine said, then he aimed his rifle and begin firing.

"Hold your fire!" Martinez shouted at the marine, and to no avail. "Hold your fire!"

The rounds flew over the horrors. Six glowing eyes stared back for just an instant then the figures scattered into the darkness. They left a gurgling torso, minus three limbs.

The marine's platoon sergeant came over to berate the breaking of noise discipline. "Who the fuck fired their weapon?" he hissed.

"Gunny, there's some fucked shit going on down there," Martinez whispered back. "We just watched some haji get taken apart." He then pointed to the dying man down the street "Check it out." Through their NVGs, they all watched the man wiggle pathetically with his one arm before succumbing to his traumatic amputation.

Even in the darkness Martinez could see Gunny's eyes narrow as his face suddenly hardened. Maybe he saw something out there that the junior marines didn't. Maybe Gunny had thoughts running through his head that he dared not say aloud. "Had to be some drugged-up insurgents going psycho," Gunny eventually said. "Just some fucked up shit."

Distinct "thumps" sounded off and Martinez saw the tell-tale flash in the far-off ruins. Explosions went off around their building. Their patrol base was under attack. Gunfire had alerted the enemy.

"Mortars! Martinez yelled out to his fellow marines. "Three hundred meters to the south!"

PART IV

The marines quickly fled the building and started moving towards the ruins. The order was made to evacuate before the insurgent forward observers could fully dial in. The last thing the marines needed was to be trapped in a building while mortars rained down on top of it. As they put in some distance, on que three mortars impacted the roof. The marines spotted on their thermals where the indirect fire had come from, and now moved quickly to close the distance.

A group of insurgents had set up two mortars about three hundred meters away. The insurgents must have thought that the fallen, collapsed structures provided enough cover, firing off their mortars into the darkness. A sudden staccato of gunfire and muzzle flashes proved them wrong.

Mortar impacts well behind them, Cpl Martinez and the rest of First Squad were moving. Approaching the ruins, they were closing in for the kill while the rest of the marines were setting up a deadly base of fire.

The insurgents returned fire in a panic. Caught off guard, they scattered across the fallen stonework as their mortars fell silent. The clacks of M16s and M249s contrasted with the metallic slams of AK-47s and a PKM.

Cpl Martinez took cover with his team behind a wall, hostile tracers shooting overhead and ripping into the old stone. Despite the chaos and under the glow of the tracers, Martinez noticed the stone looked like it was straight out of a textbook. For a fleeting moment he remembered the word "Mesopotamia," some ancient country he pretended to learn about in high school. A sudden shower of stone fragments as rounds impacted just above his head snapped him back to the fight at hand. The insurgents had to be around fifty feet away. He could hear their shouts as the insurgents barked at each other. Martinez looked at two of his marines, nodding as they all pulled a frag grenade off their flacks. They pulled their pins and all counted to three, then they let them fly. The distinct "thumps" of fragmentation grenades sounded shortly after, followed by several screams of pain. The incoming gunfire died down, and Martinez heard frantic shouts fading away. It sounded like the insurgents were falling back. Martinez peaked his head over the cover and caught sight of men indeed falling back deeper into the ruins.

Then he saw it.

The glowing eyes: three peering heads, poking over the rocks far to the left. Three sets of eyes looking right at him. Then they suddenly turned towards the fleeing insurgents. Then three forms bolted from their cover, bounding over the ground. Like a galloping dog mixed with a gorilla, they scrambled over debris; pursuing the insurgents with startling speed. A strange shrieking bark sounded. It reminded Martinez of the coyotes he would listen to back home as they hunted. It sounded like predators closing in for a kill.

"Corporal, what the fuck."

"Bro, I don't want to know," Martinez said, his heart pounding in his chest.

Gunfire and strange shrieks exploded. Screams of men soon joined the fray in a violent opera. An alien yipping filled the air. Then silence.

The marines glanced at each other.

A squad leader gave a shout and a hand signal to move forward.

A marine next to Martinez started to stammer, "No fucking way, man. I've seen how this movie ends, man. We should fall back and just call in fires on this place."

"Shut the fuck up," Martinez hissed.

First Squad moved cautiously forward, rifles at the ready, in the now-silent Fallujah dark. Signs of the battle started to appear at their feet. Shell casings littered the ground. Blood was evidence of the effectiveness of the marines' rifles.

Sure enough, Cpl Martinez saw a body lying on the ground. A military-aged male was face down. When he began to move, a wet moan broke the oppressive silence. The marines stopped and got behind cover. This wounded enemy could have friends nearby, waiting, using him like bait; a hasty ambush always a possibility.

Cpl Martinez stared down the wounded man as he stood up clutching his ruined arm. The insurgent's eyes were wide and filled with fear. He was covered in blood and Martinez saw long gashes that cut through his clothing and flesh. He frantically looked left and right before meeting Martinez's eyes in the darkness. The insurgent dropped to his knees scooping up an AK-47 with his one good arm before turning it towards Martinez. Cpl Martinez snapped his M16 to target and placed three rounds in the insurgent's chest. The man crumpled to the ground, a death rattle slipping from his lips.

As Martinez kept his eyes on the body, a sudden flutter of movement caught his attention. A figure dashed out from behind cover, sure as shit, on all fours. Before the marines could react, it had grabbed the body, and began quickly dragging it away.

This time the marines didn't hesitate.

The sound of M16's clacked after the creature and Martinez watched a few rounds impact across its body. It shrieked and dropped the body as it stumbled onto the ground. It regained its footing and turned its glowing eyes. Martinez's heart fluttered as he felt the hateful gaze of the creature, now on only him. But the thing didn't hesitate, grabbing the body as it leapt over some rubble and out of sight. The marines fired after it, but couldn't tell if they hit it again.

"What the fuck was that!?"

"Did anyone see where it went?!"

"Shut the fuck up and rifles up, marines!" Barked a squad leader. "Haji is still out there!"

"Staff Sergeant, that wasn't a fucking Haji!" A panicked marine yelled back.

"I said *shut up!* Corporal Martinez, take your team forward. Sergeant Jackson, take your team and flank left into these ruins. We're going to cover you here. You take contact: we will move up."

As Cpl Martinez moved forward with his team he took a short glance towards his squad leader; a salty staff sergeant known for his almost goofy stoicism. Martinez saw his unmistakable look of fear under the hazy green of his NVGs.

As Martinez moved forward, he heard the shaky voice

of his staff sergeant behind him say into the radio: "Atlas 26, come up on the net, we have a situation. Some...thing is out here with us. And it's not Haji."

PART V

The night was still and quiet. Nothing moved, except for Martinez. He crept forward, slowly. Fight-or-flight was firing off in his head, telling him to flee. But in the darkness he kept moving, kept seeing movement, just out of sight.

One of Martinez's marines, a man named Barnes, tapped his shoulder. "Corporal," he said, "check it out. Blood trails."

Martinez turned and, of course, he saw the dark splotches smeared on the ground.

"You think Haji dragged off their wounded?" he asked rhetorically. "Or whatever the fuck that thing we saw did?"

"Do you really want to know the answer to that, Corporal?" Barnes said aloud.

"Something tells me we are going to find out," someone else said. "It looks like the blood trails lead this way."

Cpl Martinez paused, then reached for his radio mike. "Atlas 17, this is Atlas 13. We found some blood trails. Please advise."

His radio chimed into his ear with a response, "Roger Atlas 13, follow them and make sure there aren't any squirters. We saw some movement ahead of you, looked like someone dragging a body. Atlas 12 will cover your flank. The rest of us will move up behind you. Weapons free. Atlas 17, out."

Fuck, thought Martinez. "Alright guys," he said, "we're following these trails. You see anything Haji or otherwise, fucking murk it."

"Rah, Corporal," a few said at once, then one followed it with; "safeties always off."

The four marines followed the blood like dogs on a trail. Where they found more, they found signs of fighting: shell casings, abandoned weapons, torn and shredded clothing and gear. No bodies. They even found an RPG lying on the ground, totally abandoned.

Maybe they dropped their weapons and ran, Martinez thought, but he knew better.

They had moved deeper into the ruins, fallen stone and toppled walls loomed like phantoms in the darkness. The blood trails led into a courtyard of some type; where the marines paused. Scanning carefully for movement, they saw that the blood trails ended at the base of a stone wall. Just ended, simply vanished. Martinez was considering calling it in that they had lost the trail.

Martinez and his men looked around. Ruined tombstones and memorials crowded the cramped area like crooked teeth. In the middle of these sat a large stone crypt. "We're in a graveyard," Martinez muttered, and he was sure his marines nodded. Despite the ruins around the crypt before them, it looked to be intact. Stranger still, it seemed like all the graves around it had been recently dug up. Piles of dirt and bones littered the ground. Bones littered everywhere like trash.

Why would someone dig up a graveyard? Could it have been a weapons cache?

"Martinez—," a marine screamed as he let loose with his M16, "watch out!"

Martinez turned towards a blur to his right. One of the figures had launched itself off the crypt like a missile. Its mouth was open and wide, its mammoth hands were outstretched. It was bleeding from its wounds the marines had inflicted.

Martinez couldn't raise his rifle in time as his eyes widened in horror as the creature swiped his rifle away; mouth stretched unnaturally wide. Martinez could feel its long fingers grip onto him as he fell and the creature's mouth as it began engulfing his head. But luck was on his side, and as the creature tried to crush his skull between its rancid teeth, it was caught by surprise.

Martinez, like all the marines, wore a Kevlar helmet. The damn thing was meant to prevent bullets but now stopped the creature's bite dead. The helmet held strong as the creature struggled to crush it. The creature's eyes widened and it seemed to hesitate—just long enough for Martinez to act.

He reached for the issued K-Bar knife on his vest. He quickly unsheathed it and slipped it into the creature's soft belly. Martinez screamed in terror as he stabbed and ripped into the flesh, he was covered in blood as the creature released him. It screamed in pain, swatting Martinez away, but the pain on its face turned to visible rage. It took a step towards Martinez before it stumbled back, as two of Martinez's marines dumped their mags into it. Blossoms of blood grew across its body. It screamed in pain and terror as it scrambled away from the marines, seeking shelter in the crypt as it now left its own blood trail behind.

"Corporal, are you ok!?" Barnes screamed as he bent down to lift Martinez up.

Martinez was dazed and on the verge of shock; struggling to regain his composure and footing. Fear gave way to rage. The flight response in his mind was gone, fight was all he felt now. "Where's my fucking rifle?" he growled. "Where the fuck did that thing go!?"

Barnes handed Martinez his rifle as another marine answered, "Over here, Corporal! It's in that crypt...it's not alone."

Martinez and his team trained their rifles. From within the darkness of the crypt, three pairs of glowing eyes stared back at them. He activated his IR flashlight on the end of his rifle.

Washed in the illumination, two creatures stood in front

of the wounded third as it heaved and struggled. The other two glared and hissed at the marines, baring their teeth in a disgusting but desperate grimace. Everything about them looked wrong, they were a crude mockery of nature. They were the ghouls that stalked man in his nightmares. They yipped and snapped their jaws at the marines in defiant defense, frightened animals backed into a corner.

"Fuck this," Barnes growled as he began pulling a grenade from a pouch on his flak.

Martinez followed suit as he nodded to the rest of the marines. "Frag out!"

Frag grenades were tossed into the crypt filled with growling creatures as the marines took cover. In that following silence, Martinez peeked from cover and shined down his IR. He watched as one reached down and picked up a grenade, it's face contorted into a very human curiosity. Simultaneous explosions turned them into shredded flesh in the tight confines of the crypt.

PART VI

The marines hauled ass out of the cemetery. The marines pulled security some distance away, watching the darkness for more monsters. They panted as the adrenaline pumped through their bodies. Martinez reached for his bloody radio and began to try and call for help. "Atlas 17, this is Atlas 13.

We have taken contact and need backup. Location to follow
—"

A horrifying, gurgling scream interrupted him. It was somewhere close. The marines snapped their rifles toward its direction. Maybe fifty feet away lay a mound of dirt. In its center gaped a large opening, big enough to fit a small truck through.

A bunker.

The marines had been told that Saddam had built hundreds of bunkers and miles of tunnels all over Iraq. Ammo dumps, motor pools, barracks, hangers, roads; He even buried warplanes and helicopters in the ground hidden for later use.

The source of the scream was revealed to be an Iraqi man crawling from out of the bunker. It was obvious he was one of the insurgents from earlier, the marines could observe him bleeding from gunshot wounds. On his stomach, he crawled on his hands and knees. Martinez couldn't see much, but that he was groaning and clawing into the dirt, crawling towards the marines. He raised a hand, almost in a pleading like manner, mouth open.

Before the marines could react, a long arm reached out of the darkness. It grabbed the doomed man by the ankle and pulled him back into the bunker. The marines heard a human scream, and noises of struggle before a sickening crack...followed by a disgusting tear. Then silence.

The four marines looked at each other.

Martinez spoke wearily into his radio mike, "Atlas 17, this is 13, we found a bunker of some type...I ...I think the tangos could have fled in there."

"Roger, Atlas 13, we're oscar mike to you now," the radio crackled.

Martinez's voice was shaking when he keyed the mike again, "Atlas 17, I think those things are here too."

"Roger, hold position. Anything comes out of that bunker, engage. Atlas 17, out."

Didn't have to tell him twice. Martinez kept his eyes on the entrance. If there was an abyss, he felt he was staring into it, and it was staring back at him.

"Spread the fuck out and keep your eyes on that bunker," he said to his team. "I'm going to get a better look."

They spread and took cover. Fingers were on triggers as Martinez crept closer and closer.

He could barely see anything in the darkness, but as he neared the bunker's entrance he saw movement. He paused, reaching for two IR ChemLight he kept molle'd into his flak. He cracked them, and with a quick shake, they came to life. Casting a glow invisible to the naked eye, he tossed them through the entrance, soon revealing to his NVGs a cramped tunnel.

There, in a group, several figures crouched over something; their backs turned to the entrance. They were feasting.

One ChemLight had landed at the heels of the closest ghoul, who stopped its activity and turned to stare back at Martinez.

More glowing eyes now locked on him. They all had the same faces; like the ones they'd taken out with grenades. They stared at him like those at a dinner party, having been rudely interrupted mid meal.

Cpl Martinez felt his heart beginning to thunder. Everything in his head told him to scream and start pulling the trigger. Fear, yes, but also terrifying fascination held him in place. He was out of grenades and he could count at least seven of them staring back at him.

Then the ghouls began to move slowly away, grabbing their corpses and moving deeper into the tunnel: huffing and groaning, casting glowing glances at Martinez and scowling at him as they departed.

All except one. One creature stepped forward, towards Martinez, glowing eyes locked. It stepped over the ChemLights and it was larger than the others, muscular and covered in scars.

It stopped just shy of the entrance. Keeping constant eye contact with Martinez, its face twisted into a disturbing smile, and it flung something from the tunnel which landed with a wet thud at Martinez's feet.

Martinez looked down. A human arm. He looked back up, towards the ghoul standing in the bunker. It looked almost smug.

It waved its mammoth hand and began to speak, lips contorting on its gaunt face. Its voice sounded like a twisted mockery of a human's. Cpl Martinez could make out there was language, but he didn't understand what it was saying.

It finished its speech with a final wave, then it turned and vanished, leaving Cpl Martinez and his marines in stunned silence.

PART VII

The marines would complete their mission that night, but the battle for Fallujah would continue to rage for several more days. The marines never saw the creatures again, in fact their command would pull them from all missions. The platoon was regulated to base defense, which was fine by Martinez. But when they returned from the city, they each conducted a debrief with an "intelligence specialist" who seemed to care more about the strange humanoids than the mission.

"You've seen something like this before? Haven't you?" Martinez asked the man, who only identified himself as "Barton."

The man just smiled in a way that made Martinez's blood go cold. "You can go now, Corporal."

The marines were ordered to sign Non-Disclosure

Agreements, never to discuss their odd mission under penalty of UCMJ. But they would whisper among each other about what they saw that night, a ghost story to tell in the smokepit and nothing more.

But Cpl Martinez couldn't forget about what he saw: glowing eyes and haunting smiles. Strange creatures stalked the dark corners of his dreams. He carefully asked around, risking the punishment for violating the NDA he'd signed. But he didn't care, he wanted to know what he'd seen. Were they really ghouls?

He would learn that other marines had seem something similar during Phantom Fury, strange figures that prowled the night streets of Fallujah. Ghoulish creatures that resembled twisted humans. Creatures that lived below ground, moving across Iraq in a system of tunnels and infesting Saddam's bunkers. They prayed on insurgents and civilians in the darkness. Eaters of the dead and living alike.

But what really kept him up at night, was what the creature had said to him. While he didn't understand it, the words were somehow seared into his brain. Most interpreters would wave him away once he began describing what he remembered, like they were terrified to even speak about it. The ones that were willing to listen to him could not figure out the strange language either, but pleaded with him to keep his voice down.

But soon more pressing matters, such as the ongoing

war, took his attention elsewhere.

Years later, after Fallujah and after Martinez had left the Marine Corps, he turned his search online, scouring the internet for answers. He found stories and legends of the ghouls; ancient humans who worshipped dark gods and twisted themselves into monsters. Devourers of their fellow man.

By chance, he connected with a member of a chatroom who claimed to know the language that Martinez had heard. It was Sumerian. Upon looking at the translation, Martinez snapped back to that fateful night. Seeing a ghoulish face contort as it spoke its message to him in the shadow of a burning city: "Blessings upon you for providing a feast unseen in ages."

How many times had these creatures emerged to feed on the living? In all of man's folly and conquests and wars, had these things always been there, waiting with greedy hands?

Martinez closed his computer as he took a long swig from his drink. He let the whiskey burn down his throat as he became lost in thought.

He stood and stared out the window at the uncertain dark outside, but after a few moments he began to feel unnerved and looked away. He sat back down, musing to himself. He picked up a pen and fetched his notebook as a poem came to the front of his mind:

"The eaters of the dead must dance for joy,

among the bountiful harvest,

of fields of ripe corpses,

unlike any they have seen,

nurtured in the fog of war."

THE POINTMAN

The jungle was alive. Bugs, frogs, critters; all creatures joined together in their tropical cacophony. Until suddenly— silence. A new thunder filled the air.

The rain fell like a wall from the heavens. A damp, oppressive curtain that soaked into every pore and crack leaving no place for sanctuary from the downfall. The rain swapped the oppressive jungle heat for a suffocating humidity, creating a haze that draped a sinister cloak over that hellscape.

A man stalked forward, crouched low to the ground, each step deliberate, and soft into the quickly dampening mud. He held an M16, slick from the rain, in his pruned, callused hands. A gold embroidered patch, resembling a crimson leaf bearing a lightning bolt, adorned his left shoulder. He was following the path of least resistance, hoping that this was a path well-traveled. Thinking like his enemy. A hunter after the most dangerous prey.

His eyes were wild from exhaustion and adrenaline. A junkie addicted by force. His eyes scanned left to right. Up and down. His ears strained for any sound out of place in the pouring rain. He sniffed the air, hoping to sense some sign. He soaked in all his senses could muster. His uniform was a soaping mess; ruined and destroyed from weeks out in the field. Web gear chafed him raw, but he kept it tight to him, preventing any noise while he moved. The jungle was the last place the twenty-two-year-old from the mean streets of Detroit ever expected to find himself. But after months in country, he was a natural moving within it. It felt like home.

He stopped and took a knee. Though his olive-drab boonie was soaked to its brim, instinctively he reached up and wiped the sweat and rain from his brow.

"Stop. Look down."

He shifted his gaze to the ground before him, scanning slowly, cautiously; looking for a hidden danger he now knew was there.

"The stone...do you see the pattern on the leaves?"

Sergeant Josiah Blackburn locked his eyes on a curious stone. It sat out of place in the middle of his path, and there were no other stones like it. In fact, there were no stones around him at all. It was a river stone, precariously placed on the jungle ground. To the right of it was a pile of leaves that looked too perfect, too deliberate to be happenstance. He unsheathed his bayonet and slowly inched forward. Carefully he began to poke the bayonet into the mud, there could be a mine or something waiting to be triggered. The last thing he wanted was a face full of shrapnel or to be impaled by some grotesque bamboo trap.

He moved, even slower, feeling for any resistance or something other than jungle mud. So far nothing solid. He slipped the blade just under the outer array of leaves and began to wiggle its tip. He lifted it ever so slightly and the mass of leaves rose. Reaching forward and grabbing a hold of the net hidden under the leaves, he pulled. The leaves had been sown together: a makeshift camo net. It had been covering a hole; a good four-feet-deep hole, wide enough for a man to stand in.

Blackburn looked down into the deadfall and could only admire with grim respect the ingenious of it. A simple camo net disguised to look like refuse on the jungle floor covering a hole. An unassuming step would have sent him falling feet first onto a dozen wooden stakes sharpened to deadly points. A trap like this would have turned his feet and legs into Swiss cheese. If he was lucky he'd bleed out in minutes, if he was unlucky the trap would immobilize him and turn him into deadweight. To add insult to injury, the smell wafting up suggested that the muck waiting at the bottom wasn't just mud; mixing that with your blood would guarantee a nasty infection...if you made it out of the jungle at all.

Blackburn tossed the camo net aside. He reached into his cargo pocket and pulled out a length of white engineer tape. Carefully laying it on the ground, he made an X shape on either side of the deadfall. His platoon, who carefully followed his footsteps some one hundred meters back, he knew they'd appreciate this heads up.

A trap like this could also mean something else...

"You're not alone."

He quickly sidestepped from the deadfall taking cover behind a log. He peered through the haze and rain, scanning for an unseen foe.

"They haven't noticed you yet. The rain is too thick."

Josiah had been in Vietnam for six months now, that whole while a member of a Long-Range Surveillance team. LRS had put him on countless missions; deep behind enemy lines. Hard lessons had taught him many of the Vietcong's tricks. He had a reputation for his seemingly keen sense of where and what Charlie was working—hence why he was on point for his platoon right now. His platoon mates held him in high regard as a tracker and point man. They all believed he had a sixth sense or something, and that it would keep them alive and breathing, their flesh free of bullets, and their feet unpunctured by vile bamboo.

If only they really knew, he mused to himself as his platoon crept behind, fascinated by "the pointman."

If he was a betting man, that deadfall was simply a distraction. Charlie was nearby, probably waiting for some hapless GI to fall into that shit-filled pit. The screams would alert more GIs, who would come to his aid, which in turn would tell the Viet Cong their trap had been sprung.

Blackburn cursed himself under his breath. How could he have been so stupid, sitting out there in the open for so long? He was lucky that the rain was falling and, in turn, had created a jungle fog. That and the fact he was alone probably saved him. Charlie was nearby, but he hadn't fallen for their trap nor had he been seen. But that wasn't going to last for long. Soon the fifty-two soldiers behind were going to catch up, and fifty-two GIs moving through the jungle was going to be hard to hide.

"There's only two of them."

Good. That means just a rearguard, Blackburn thought. An unknown-sized element of VC had bloodied a patrol in an ambush not far from here; the same group had allegedly shot down the medevac bird that came to retrieve the wounded. Blackburn's platoon was selected for a search and destroy mission: to eliminate this group with prejudice. Intel had determined that this group was made up of veteran fighters; they knew the Americans were coming for them.

They most likely were counting on this ambush to buy them enough time to vanish deeper into the jungle.

"In front of you."

The rain was beginning to lighten and the fog beginning to dissipate. Blackburn scanned to his right, and he saw it. A fighting position sat about one hundred feet in front of him. It was a half crescent of dirt with palm fronds and large leaves thrown over it. The unmistakable barrel of a RPD light machine gun protruded out between a gap in its dirt. The position was off the trail, but it would block the platoon from moving forward.

"Look to your right. Follow the path."

The rain suddenly picked back up. Fat raindrops fell like artillery, drowning out the noise in the jungle with a steady roar. Blackburn quickly understood. The brush got thick to his right and a fallen tree provided concealment. However, there was a break in the thick vegetation, most likely a trail used by some native fauna...and by the Vietcong. He sheathed his bayonet and got low to the ground, he had to move quick before his platoon caught up. He didn't have time to warn them or wait. They would either run into the trap or he would run the risk of alerting their enemy. He crept deeper into the jungle now, following the natural path that weaved its way between thick vegetation and the trunks of trees. He knew where the path would take him.

Soon he reached his destination as he took cover behind

a towering tree. The jungle path had led him to a position right behind the machine gun nest. Blackburn could make out two men laying in the prone under a makeshift canopy of leaves.

The impacts of rain on the foliage created a gentle thunder, and Blackburn crept forward, towards his targets. He gently slung his M16 across his back, carefully tightening the sling so the rifle would'nt flop around and generate noise. He didn't want to start shooting to only to have his platoon gun him down by accident. He would have to do this the hard way.

Blackburn unsheathed his bayonet once more and held it in an icepick grip. He crept closer and paused some ten feet away from the nest, holding his breath, remaining motionless in the rain.

"The one on the left is asleep."

He crept closer and closer until he was almost on top of the nest. The rain fell in a roar and thunder boomed overhead, but he could only hear the beating of his own heart. He could clearly see the two men in front of him now. Blackburn readied his blade and made his moved.

Blackburn lunged and fell upon the man behind the machine gun. Blackburn plunged his bayonet into the base of his enemy's neck. Skin and muscle gave way as the blade struck the spine. Blackburn felt the blade slide to the right along the spine into the meat of the neck, he twisted the edge and ripped it to the right. Blood squirted in a sickening spectacle. The surprised man struggled, and in the throes of this death, Blackburn followed up with three quick stabs.

"His friend is awake."

Blackburn pivoted and jumped, diving at the Vietcong whose face was beginning to contort in shock and horror. Blackburn's bayonet slid home, into the ribcage of this second man. Blackburn kicked the rifle out of the doomed Vietcong's hands as he brought it up to bare. Blackburn stabbed and stabbed until the man stopped moving.

"He's dead. You can stop now."

The pointman sheathed his bayonet and unslung his rifle. The rain was subsiding. He stood over the dead men, covered in their blood, panting. And he heard a shout.

"Your platoon can see you."

"Dole!" a shadowy figure shouted from behind a tree.

"I'd kill for a pineapple now!" Blackburn shouted back. "In fact, two Charlie KIA."

Blackburn's lieutenant ran up as the rest of the LRS platoon emerged, forming a perimeter.

"I don't have a pineapple, sergeant. I hope a cigarette will do." The LT half-smiled, passing a cigarette to Blackburn before taking one out for himself. The platoon leader lit the pointman's before lighting his own. The LT took a drag and surveyed the bodies and the nest, nudging the RPD with his foot. "Damn," he said, "we would have walked right up on these two. They could have done a number on us if you didn't catch that deadfall and get the drop. You're really something...or you just have the best damn luck."

Blackburn wished it was luck. He sat down next to the first man he'd killed; those eyes beginning to glaze over, staring lifeless up at the canopy. Blackburn watched the life fully leave his eyes before he closed his own and took a long drag. Death had become something he was intimately familiar with. He looked up into the jungle, "I don't know, sir. I guess you could say I got a 'guardian angel' of sorts. He won't let me die out here."

The LT chuckled, tossing his cigarette onto the body of the dead machine gunner. "Either way, good job, sergeant. Catch your breath, we're moving out in ten."

Sergeant Josiah Blackburn stared into the jungle, meeting eyes with his "guardian angel" who crouched just a few feet in front from him. A pale face and glazed eyes of a murdered thirteen-year-old boy met his from the thick underbrush.

That was his secret, the "six sense" as his platoon said. It was how he was able to sniff out every trap and foil every ambush the Vietcong tried to set. It's how he kept them all alive. He was owed many lives and more beers than he could count. It's how he, Josiah Blackburn, stayed alive.

Was it real? He didn't know. He would never actually admit to his fellows and leadership that he was "seeing a ghost." Trust in combat is a path walked on a razors edge. In Nam, survival was always in doubt, you needed to trust the man to your left and right with every fiber of your being. He had seen how that could fall apart the minute people began to doubt each other. The jungle is a land of wolves. No sane many wanted to trust someone who couldn't even trust their mind. So, the pointman kept his mouth shut, his secret unknown to all but him. After all, maybe it was just blind luck…and insanity?

But insanity and war made dangerous bedfellows.

On the wrong side of town, Detroit had been a lot like Vietnam. A kid on the edge of poverty with parents who cared more about their next drink than their two sons sleeping on the floor of their dirty apartment. As a result, Josiah and his older brother, Martin, were often on their own. The future pointman's older brother was as much a parent as he was a brother. A man far before he should have been, Martin regularly reassured Josiah with a simple phrase: "I'm your guardian angel."

Those words were a whisper in the back of his mind, they haunted the pointman's silence. After hiding the bodies, the platoon crept away from the dead VC, but they didn't creep far before establishing their patrol base before it got dark. That night Josiah dreamed the same dream he had every night since he'd come to Nam, a nightmare on repeat every time he closed his eyes. Two unsupervised boys our after midnight, stealing cigarettes then selling them for pennies outside seedy bars. A night like many others, until they were suddenly fleeing for their lives through the back alleys of the city. A dead end, and Martin shoving a terrified Josiah into a trashcan. Martin hissing at him to keep quiet as he closed the lid. The angry shouts of a struggle, the terrified and desperate voice of his brother. A ghastly gurgle.

Then there was silence.

Josiah stayed in that reeking trashcan until daylight, tears and urine collecting at the bottom of his protection. When he finally discovered the courage to emerge, the alley was empty except for the ruined body of his brother. A pale face drained of blood and glazed eyes stared into his face as Josiah heard from nowhere and everywhere, *"Let me take care of you."*

"Wake up."

"Sergeant," Sgt Blackburn awoke to someone shaking his shoulder, "it's your turn to pull security." Blackburn opened his eyes to a red flashlight, sounds of a jungle night refilling his ears. A full moon was still painting the bush in its white. The dream had begun to fade.

He looked at the soldier who'd woke him, giving him a pat on the shoulder. Blackburn rolled over and reached for his canteen. Taking a swig of lukewarm water, he settled back into the prone of his fighting position. The platoon was set up not far from where Blackburn had killed the two

Vietcong. The LT had hoped their friends would come looking for them eventually. The men's blood had blended with the filth and sweat of Blackburn's uniform, another memory stained upon the pointman's soul. A soldier next to him was awake; kneeling next to his ruck, searching for something under the dull red of his flashlight.

"They can see him."

"Get down!" Blackburn moved quickly, grabbing the soldier and jerking him to down. A burst of gunfire ruptured. Tracers shot over their heads.

"Contact!" someone yelled.

An RPG sailed over Blackburn, impacting behind him. Another machine gun opened up, its muzzle flash like lightning.

"I'm hit!" screamed someone else in the dark.

"Man down! Man Down!" a soldier yelled frantically.

"Medic!" pleaded another.

"Enemy fire to the north!" the LT shouted above the chaos.

As bullets flew overhead, someone came walking up on Sgt Blackburn's left. He didn't need to look to know who it was. A voice spoke softly.

"They are in front of you, fifty of them."

The pointman yelled out, "Contact at my twelve o' clock! Platoon-sized element, two hundred meter!" Blackburn hugged the dirt and returned fire with his M16, letting off several bursts towards the muzzle flashes in front of him. He looked to his left and then to his right and saw more muzzle flashes suddenly blossoming within the jungle. The numbers weren't looking good. Luckily, the vegetation and the hasty fighting positions the Americans had dug provided enough cover and concealment.

The M60 next to Blackburn opened up as its gunner fed the pig. The heavy slams of its receiver were like thunderclaps as red tracers cut into the jungle. More M16s joined the fray. Several "thumps" from M79 grenade launchers resulted in bursts of light and shrapnel along the lines.

"Holy shit, we really kicked the hornets' nest, Blackburn!" grinned the soldier whom he'd saved, a cocky southern boy with a crooked smile. "Can't wait to tell the girls at *Trigger Jacks* this war story," he laughed. A bullet then entered his skull and destroyed it in a shower of blood. The pointman reached out to him, gasping.

"Don't bother, he's dead."

Blackburn stopped himself and refocused down the sights of his rifle. He didn't give a second glance, what was done was done.

A shrill whistle rose above the gunfire, and a roar of yells followed suite. Several illumination flares went up into the sky, painting the jungle in a dull bluish light. Men started to emerge, running and firing madly. He put his sights over a man in black pajamas and pulled the trigger. A bark and a flash and the man fell, but soon more appeared behind him. The Vietcong were charging the patrol base. It was becoming plain to Blackburn that the platoon was outnumbered. But as it seemed they were going to overrun their positions, and explosion of dirt and fire appeared all around them. Artillery fire. Danger close.

A cry of "Fall Back!" sounded over the gunfire and several men repeated it.

Blackburn got up and started hauling ass to his fallback position, more explosions beginning to slam around him. The rounds were landing too close, practically on top of the Americans. Blackburn sprinted as fast as he could as dirt and sparks rose from the earth in geysers. A whistle suddenly filled his ears and he found himself rising into the air.

Not rising. Flying. Flung by a wayward arty round. He landed on his back. He couldn't feel anything nor could he move. His ears rang in shell-shocked silence. He turned his head and saw that his leg was lying next to him, an amputated piece of flesh. His vision began to fade into darkness. But above the ringing he heard that familiar voice whisper:

"You won't die today."

Josiah Blackburn awoke days later. At first he thought he was dead, and this was finally heaven. He looked around and saw the rows of hospital beds and ruined men he was still in Vietnam. *So that had to mean hell or maybe purgatory,* he thought, but he knew he wasn't that lucky.

He tried to get up and the shock of pain reminded him he was very much still alive. He fell back into the pillow, wincing in pain. He felt around with his hands: he was heavily stitched up and bandaged across his abdomen and torso. He remembered seeing his leg lying right next to him. He looked down and his heart skipped a beat, a bandaged stub revealed his leg really was gone. The pain now was starting to radiate throughout his whole body, as if it now suddenly remembered it was in, indeed, pain.

A nurse noticed he was awake and writhing. Soon he was swarmed by orderlies. The morphine they gave him put him back into a blissful sleep.

Sometime later he awoke. He was propped up now with a steady morphine drip in an IV. He glanced around and noticed he was now alone. Truly alone. No ghostly image of a dead boy keeping him company. No voice whispering to him that only he could hear. Maybe it really was all in his head. It was a strange feeling, and without the constant specter of Martin, he felt vulnerable.

A familiar voice caught his attention. "Blackburn! They told me you were waking up. I came as quick as I could." His platoon leader was walking towards him.

"The fellas wanted to come to, but these docs are only letting first sergeants and above visit. They wanted me to give you these." His platoon leader handed Blackburn a stack of magazines and a carton of cigarettes. "It's good to see you awake, I didn't think you were going to make it out of there."

"Thanks, sir," Blackburn said, accepting the gifts. He lifted up a news magazine to see that the stack was primarily of the pornographic kind. He smiled as he slipped them under his covers. "What happened, sir?"

The lieutenant looked down. "Well, after our artillery decided to drop rounds on top of us, we fell back as Charlie did." He stared at the floor, "When we regrouped we were all pretty torn up. We were almost overrun and we had to retreat. Leave you behind."

The lieutenant turned and wiped a tear away. For a brief moment, he seemed stared off into another please, before sighing and regained himself. "Charlie," he said, "tried to counterattack again but they retreated once the shells started landing right. We took our chances and retreated back to the rally point."

The lieutenant paused and silence between the two men soured the air.

"I thought I died, sir," Blackburn said.

The lieutenant chuckled, "Me too. And then the strangest thing happened."

Blackburn was puzzled, "What do you mean?"

The lieutenant looked around, nervously. Then he got closer and lowered his voice to a whisper. "We heard a voice, a kid's voice, yell *Hey!* behind us. And not a Vietnamese one. This voice was good old American. All of us whipped around, and there was this kid just standing in the jungle, just feet behind us."

Blackburn stuttered as his heart began to beat faster and his stomach dropped.

"It was a kid, man, he looked like he was plucked off the street back home and dropped in the jungle."

Blackburn felt his throat begin to tighten.

"But before we could say anything, he fucking vanished. Like one minute he was there and the next he was gone. Like he was made of mist. We all saw him."

Josiah felt like he wanted to throw up.

"And there you were, bleeding and battered. Torniquet on your leg. But no one claimed to have carried you, no one saw what had happened to you. You were missing that leg and there's no way you could've crawled to us."

Blackburn felt the color leaving his face as he stared up at the ceiling of the tent. He was breaking into a sweat.

The lieutenant continued, "We ran up to you and you were still breathing. The medics did what they could and we moved like hell to get you on a bird. You were torn the fuck up, Blackburn...which, I guess, you know. I didn't know if you were going to make it."

The LT got up and put a hand on Blackburn's shoulder, "We just all chalked it up to a miracle. Your guardian angel coming through for you."

The pointman said nothing.

The lieutenant patted him on the shoulder. "Get some rest, Blackburn. You earned it." The lieutenant left and soon Blackburn was alone.

Sergeant Josiah Blackburn laid in his hospital bed unmoving and in silence. So much was running through his head. He didn't know what to think.

But then he felt something on his hand. As he felt a chill come over his body, he refused to turn and look. He shook his head in denial.

But it was one cold hand, embracing another. And he heard the voice whisper:

"I'm your guardian angel."

REUNION

He began to panic.

This was supposed to be a fun weekend, one of play and games. A weekend with his family, a weekend about them. Not about the past and the pain that welled up every weekend such as this one, the type of pain he once looked to drown in the bottom of a bottle. The type of pain that had almost robbed him of his family and his life.

He had taken his seven-year-old daughter away from the campsite, leaving his wife and their youngest behind to nap under the shade of swaying pines. He wasn't worried to leave them behind, his own mother and father kept them company by the fireside. He wanted to go fishing, but his little girl wouldn't leave his hip. She always wanted to be with her daddy. He called her his "little shadow."

The two of them walked away, skirting the river. Thirty minutes later, they picked a secluded place and searched for a spot to cast a line into the babbling waters from the banks. She was more interested in looking for worms and rocks, and he let her wander if she promised to stay close. He didn't think anything of it, they were the only ones he had seen out here. He welcomed this return to nature. His mind, sharpened by the anxiety of combat, felt at peace.

As he waded up to his ankles, he soon lost himself in the tranquility of it all. The soothing current of the river calmed him as he searched for an unlucky trout. So lost in the blissful moments was he, he soon realized he didn't hear little giggles and sounds of play. He turned around.

His daughter was gone.

The flowing waters were no longer peaceful, they were raging rapids in his ears. He ran through sloshing water closer to shore and called out her name, waiting in desperate hope for a response.

Nothing.

He yelled some more, looking left and right. He walked up into the brush along the bank. Nothing. He began to look and scream her name. He did this relentlessly, each second becoming more frantic then the last. But she was nowhere to be seen.

That's it. She's gone. She's fucking gone, a panicked voice repeated in his head. The same voice that haunted him, fed on his guilt, prodded him to anger, and that whispered in his nightmares. He fought off the voice, trying to push it away. Hyperventilating, he put his hands on his head. His knees began to weaken, and he felt he couldn't stand.

That voice started to get louder. He had no cell service. Should he run for help? Leave the spot where he last saw her? He began to imagine the panicked look on his pregnant wife's face; her eyes welling in fear as the infant in her arms began to wail. He couldn't dare himself to confront her. To tell her what had just happened.

To admit he didn't know what to do. That he had failed. That someone who he cared about was gone. Again.

The damn was breaking, and the flood was nigh.

The silence of the forest was interrupted by the haunting sound of a sobbing man.

For an endless number of moments, he cried. Grief, shame, agony mixing together in a dark storm upon his soul. But over his sobs, he heard something. The high-pitched squeak of a girl.

"Daddy?"

He looked up and the storm was broken. His little girl was emerging from the bushes, running back into the safety of his arms. A surge of anger flashed through him as she returned to him, fueled by parental frustrations. But like a flash of lighting, it has there and gone as he felt a euphoric relief. He grabbed her in an embrace and determined to never let go. He held her out to take a look at her.

"Alexis, what happened!? Where did you go?"

He looked her over, she seemed no worse for the wear. Dirty from the forest. Just the look of a concerned and scared little girl. "Sweetheart, what happened?"

Tears began to well up in those beautifully innocent brown eyes. In between the gasping sobs of a child, he picked up details. She had chased butterflies into the woods, ignoring her fathers warning to stay close, straying away from the river, and out of sight. She hadn't seen the sudden drop into a ravine, tumbling down the steep slopes.

His anger got the better of him. He had specifically told her to stay close, that the woods could be dangerous if she wasn't careful. His face began to harden. Poorly buried demons began to claw out from their cages. Barking and howling. Ones that craved and feasted on anger. Ones that were born long ago to run free on a battlefield that he had left behind. Demons that had almost destroyed his marriage and almost ended his life. But that was a story for another time.

His hands grasped his daughters shoulders a little tighter, his face poorly concealing his growing anger.

His little girl took a dirty hand to her face, wiping away the snot and tears. "Daddy, I'm sorry I made you mad…"

The demon's howling turned to a pitiful whine. He felt

his heart break. He embraced her. How could *he* have been so careless, so angry at himself that he projected it on her. Shame washed away the anger.

"I'm not mad at you," he soothed. "Daddy just got scared."

He regained his composure and stood up, still holding her close. He silenced those demons that threatened to destroy him once again. But his hackles went back up as he scanned into the woods with suspicious eyes. Every swaying branch suddenly seemed potentially dangerous now. He wouldn't let something like this happen again.

"Let's go back to the camp," he said ushering her along. "I think it's time to get some s'mores."

And with this a small smile returned to her face.

His daughter clutching on to him, he turned and began to head back to their campsite.

Alexis began to wiggle in his arms, "But Daddy, aren't you going to wait for your friend?"

He stopped and looked her in the eyes. "What are you talking about, sweetheart?"

"Your friend, Daddy! He said he was your best friend!"

"Daddy's friends didn't come out to camp with us, sweetheart."

She had a puzzled look on her face. "But he said he was one of your Army friends."

Those hackles went up again. *A man? In the woods?* He

scanned the now ominous woods with hardened eyes.

He put Alexis down and took a knee, coming eye level with her. He placed both hands on her shoulders. "Sweetheart, please tell Daddy what happened. Who was this man?"

She looked shyly at the ground and then at something behind him. "He was right there, Daddy," she eventually said. He turned around, but nothing was there.

"I fell down the big hill but then your friend grabbed my hand and picked me up and carried me up the big hill!"

He looked at her.

"The man said he was your friend, and that he was going to take me back to you. And he held my hand."

She paused to wipe the remaining snot from her nose.

"We walked back to you, and he told me about how you and he went on adventures!" She suddenly held a look of excitement. "Can you tell me about your Army adventures, Daddy?"

He didn't know what to think. "Sweetheart," he said, "what did this man look like?"

"Ummmm, he had dark hair, and his skin was brown, he had a gap in his front teeth like me—oh, he wore the same clothes like your old job, in those pictures you showed me!"

His eyes grew wide.

"He pointed here," she continued, pointing to the right side of her chest, "and said his name was Ricardo. But I could call him Mr. Ricky. And that he was so happy to finally meet me."

He kneeled in silence. A war waged in his stomach. He could never forget that name. That was the name inscribed on the black bracelet he wore on his wrist.

SSG RICARDO "RICKY" DANIEL
OPERATION ENDURING FREEDOM
29MAY09

She smiled. "Mr. Ricky, he is always with you he said. You just don't know it sometimes."

His hands began to tremble. "Sweetheart, are you sure?"

"Yes, Daddy. He was right behind us."

He stood up and turned around, scanning the foliage. Looking at every shadow, every twitch, for something. Anything. Cold sweat travelled down his face.

"There, Daddy—look! Hi, Mr. Ricky!"

A man stood next to a tree, a soldier in a faded Army Combat Uniform. The soldier stared at them before breaking into a toothy smile.

He knew that smile anywhere. He held the soldier's gaze in disbelief before breaking into a sad smile and a nod. The soldier nodded back and waved before turning and walking into the shadows of the forest.

Father and daughter both watched as he faded away. As

he vanished, a gentle breeze embraced both of them.

"Goodbye Mr. Ricky," Alexis said. He again picked up his daughter up in his arms. Walking slowly in silence as she held onto him tightly.

Memories of friendship, brotherhood, war, and tragedy replayed in his heart. Memories that he had allowed to spoil to the point of becoming pain. Whispers and demons retreated deep into his mind. He looked up into the sky and smiled.

"Sweetheart, I want to tell you about someone."

THE TAKING OF CLYDESDALE 66

NOW

When Chief Warrant Officer Percy Diaz opened her eyes, the first thing that ran through her head was the beauty of the stars.

Crickets chirped around her, enhancing her bliss with their violins. A cold mountain wind blew, gently, caressing her cheek as it rustled the tall grass in which she lay. She laid on her back; in awe of the Milky Way and the near-infinite stars. It was like a painting—no, a masterpiece; on display across the vast night sky. She couldn't remember the last time she saw a night like this, and her eyes were wide as she watched her breath form into a cloud rising into the air.

She thought back to her childhood, reminiscing fondly of a stargazing youth. Her heart filled with joy and wonder. She used to imagine that, one day, she would fly into that same night that she was in awe of. A smile was growing across her face.

And then it hit her.

She jolted back into reality, heart racing, sitting up. Her heart pounded against her ribs as she looked around her.

Diaz jumped to her feet and drew her service pistol from her flight vest: a useless gesture in the pitch darkness of the Afghanistan night.

"Where the fuck am I?" she muttered. She realized she was still wearing her flight helmet, and with a relief reached up to bring down her PVS14s over her eyes.

Suddenly her vision replaced darkness for the ghostly, blueish gray. Through her night vision goggles, the mountains of Afghanistan loomed. She was in a field surrounded by hills, filled with tall grass, somewhere far from any semblance of civilization that could be found in Nuristan. A cold wind blew, rustling the grass around her. She looked in every direction, trying to understand.

"Where the fuck *am* I?" she growled, mind alight in disorientation. Then she remembered her crew. "Bazgew!" she yelled, "Hernandez! Chu! Anyone!?"

What the fuck is happening? Diaz wondered. She couldn't remember how she'd got here.

And as she tried, her head erupted with a splitting migraine. It was like she had been struck in the head. It was as if the attempt to remember had set her brain now on fire.

She dropped to a knee as the pain became unbearable. Her weapon fell from her hands as she reflexively grabbed at her head. An earsplitting sound erupted in the confines of her skull, like nails on a chalkboard combined with explosive static. An inhuman scream was rending through her brain. She tried to brace through the pain, her jaw clenched with such force she felt she would break it.

As the pain contorted her, her abdomen suddenly clinched in a tell-tale sign of what would happen next. Diaz fell to all fours as she vomited uncontrollably. As the last of the bile cleared her throat, the pain in her head began to subside.

Diaz tasted blood in her mouth.

The head fog began to lift and images flashed through her mind. Panic began to fracture her attempt at staying calm. Coughing and trying to catch her breath, she struggled to remember what the fuck was going on. Where was she? How did she get here? What happened?

A strange metallic hum rose above the wind, snapping Percy out of her thoughts. She couldn't remember much, but she did remember she was on her own...in the wild west of Afghanistan. Taliban territory. She reached out and recovered her pistol, gripping it tightly in the darkness.

Diaz looked up through her NVGs and spied a large rock sitting among the tall grass. She crawled to it on her hands and knees, sitting up and bracing her back against it. She panted as she tried to catch her breath. She laid her pistol in her lap and looked into the night sky again, this time through her NVGs. The stars above were infinite.

She grabbed at the memories coming back. Struggling to solve the puzzle racing through her mind. She went back to the beginning.

Six Hours Ago

Chief Warrant Officer Percy Diaz walked across the Bagram flightline. As she made her way to her UH60 Blackhawk, she glanced around. In the fading twilight, the airfield was alive with movement. She walked past several soldiers working on aircraft spread out on the flight line, the maintenance never ceased on helicopters, they ate parts and were always hungry for more. A trio of Apache gunships galloped in, their empty rocket pods and absent hellfire missiles told Diaz all she needed to know about the success of their hunt. Two F15's screamed down the runway before climbing near vertical into the sky; *either the pilots are showing off or they just scrambled for a mission,* Diaz thought to herself as she walked to her helicopter.

Soon, Diaz sipped an energy drink as she set her gear

down onto her seat. She had just finished her flight brief and was wired for tonight's mission. She was the pilot in command tonight, and she looked forward to the flight hours.

Diaz and her crew had been tasked to fly a resupply to a lone outpost tucked away in the Nuristan National Forest Reserve. Flying in at night to drop off rations and mail attracted a lot less attention than flying over the Taliban's head during the day.

While she was closing out her brief, her crew had been working on the preflight for their aircraft. Diaz's copilot, First Lieutenant Bazgew, was busily fiddling with the radios and the navigation system.

"Alright, Brandon," Diaz teased. "I'm trusting you to not get us lost. You know what they say about LTs."

"Yeah, yeah, can't spell lost without LT," Bazgew chuckled back.

Her crew chiefs, Specialist Chu and Sergeant Hernandez, they were busy mounting the aircrafts two M240 machine guns. While they had the speed of the aircraft and their skills to avoid fire, the ability to send one thousand rounds of 7.62mm back at the enemy was the preferred method to deal with contact.

"Chief, take the scenic route?" Sgt Hernandez asked. "Flight's going to be boring anyways."

"Yeah, I was kind of hoping to fire off this thousand rounds," Chu added excitedly.

Diaz slapped the side of the helicopter and laughed, "Even Haji has to sleep, you guys."

Their battalion had been in country for five months now. For many, including her entire crew, this was their first taste of Afghanistan. This was Diaz's second deployment to the country; she had flown hundreds of hours in hostile skies, had taken fire more times than she could count, and had even more close calls in the air.

As a cold wind blew across the flight line, Diaz was thankful for her winter flight gear. Still, she shivered just a bit under her Army-issued layers. It was more nerves than the cold, of course. The wind was a reminder of how hostile these skies could be. It had brought down plenty of aircraft without the assistance of the Taliban. Luckily, at this point in her career, she was able to mask her apprehension before every mission.

Hopefully, at least for tonight, this flight should be a simple one. It was winter and typically the Taliban went to ground to build their strength for the spring offensives. That combined with a late-night hit time at the outpost should mean for a relatively quit ride. But flight missions over Afghanistan could provide a slew of surprises.

Diaz watched the twilight fade as more and more stars appeared and twinkled. It was a clear night tonight; not a cloud. Diaz gulped down the small knot in her throat, putting her flight helmet on and then activating her NVGs. It was time to get in the air. She clapped her hands together. "Alright, fellas. Let's get this show on the road."

The crew quickly prepped for launch, tying down the cargo and finishing radio checks. Diaz and her copilot ran through their preflight checklist, robotically going step by step as had been drilled into them after countless hundreds of hours of training. Soon a sharp whine erupted from the aircraft as it began to power up. The frame began to rock as the four blades began to turn; slowly at first, then they were a blur and the whine had become a roar.

Diaz and Bazgew finished their final checks and radioed for clearance to taxi as their crew chiefs secured themselves in the Blackhawk. Their request was granted and they slowly began to rise off the ground. The aircraft hovered to its takeoff point. They hovered for a few minutes for some final checks before the tower told them to standby for traffic. Diaz brought down the aircraft to allow a massive C17 laden with soldiers returning home begin its slow rumble down the runway. The crew watched the massive gray aircraft soon rise into the sky.

Four more months and that will be us heading home Diaz thought to herself. The Blackhawk took its place on the flight line and waited eagerly for its turn.

"Tower, this is Clydesdale 66, request clearance for takeoff," Diaz chimed into the radio.

A man's voice chimed back. "Roger that, Clydesdale 66,

you are cleared for takeoff. Stay safe out there."

Diaz took a breath and the Blackhawk thundered down the runway, rising ever higher. As the aircraft cleared the runway, it turned to follow the course Bazgew had programmed into their navigation system. Below them, Afghanistan had gone dark. The farther they got from Bagram, the less signs of people they saw. But luckily the sky remained open, and the innumerable stars provided enough ambient light.

As Diaz wrestled with the wind, she stole a look at those stars. Out here, without the light pollution and her NVGs, Diaz could see everything. The Milky Way was in full view, and Diaz couldn't help but admire.

"Holy shit, check that out!" Bazgew pointed as a meteor came thundering from the heavens.

Diaz watched the extraterrestrial projectile rocket down on the same course they were on. It was a strange, but beautiful sight: a streaking object cutting across the sky. The two pilots watched as it plummeted to earth over the mountains. A flash ominously followed and moments after it all vanished from view.

"Chief, you think it crashed into the mountains out there?" Bazgew asked. "Maybe we'll find a kryptonian in a crater."

They neared the mountain range, and as they did Diaz increased altitude. The Blackhawk began to shudder and groan in the thin air.

"Not sure, LT, but let's make sure we don't," Diaz responded back dryly. "Crash, that is."

The Blackhawk jumped and shook. Diaz and Bazgew wrestled the controls as they maneuvered deeper through the mountains, flying between peaks and over ridgelines in the starlit dark.

Soon, a small outpost nestled in a valley came into view.

"Paladin CP, this is Clydesdale 66, approaching DZ Hospice," Diaz called out on her radio.

"Roger, Clydesdale 66, read you Lima Charlie," a static-fuzzed voice responded. "Confirm you see the DZ."

Diaz looked through her NVGs at a clearing situated in the middle of a series of Hescos. A soldier stood in the center of the clearing, swinging an IR ChemLight in a large circle.

"Confirmed."

The Blackhawk began its rapid descent. While Diaz hoped the Taliban were asleep, she knew the reality was they were probably watching this outpost. An outpost surrounded on all sides by the high ground. A helicopter would be a prime target for a mortar or a RPG team.

Chu and Hernandez were busy preparing in the back, the helicopter wouldn't be long on the helipad. Diaz slowed the Blackhawk as it got closer, soon touching down as a wall of dust browned out the crew's vision. Diaz reduced power to the engines as the dust cloud dissipated.

A group of infantrymen ran towards the aircraft, setting

up a human chain in the dark. They hurriedly grabbed the boxes of rations and mail that Chu and Hernandez shoved towards them. The aircraft was emptied in less than a minute and the infantrymen retreated off the helipad as a dust cloud exploded upwards.

Diaz increased power, rising up and away from the outpost as it turned to exit the valley.

"Delivery complete, Paladin CP, goodnight and see you later."

"Roger that, Clydesdale 66, thanks. Safe flying. Paladin CP, out."

The Blackhawk once again fought the thin mountain air as it rose over the high ground. The crew chiefs peered out from behind their machine guns: it appeared the Taliban were in fact asleep.

The Blackhawk increased altitude over the peaks. The rest of the flight should be quiet before they returned home.

With the outpost thirty minutes behind them, the crew diverted their course to a FARP located at a combat outpost outside Bagram to refuel before the final leg of their journey. They had all the time their fuel levels would allow them now.

Diaz turned to Bazgew and prompted her copilot, "Hey, LT, on the job training is the best type of training. I'm handing off the stick to you. Three...Two...O—"

"Hey, Chief, wait—do you see that?" Bazgew interrupted. "Ahead of us. Eleven o'clock. What the fuck is that?"

Diaz looked up and ahead. She strained her eyes.

A bright light flashed in the darkness below. A blue light lit up the interior of the Blackhawk. Diaz closed her eyes, not wanting to be blinded by her NVGs.

"Shit, I can't see!" Bazgew shouted as the aircraft jerked.

Diaz squinted, struggling to regain her own vision. She shouted, "I got stick, I got stick!"

Diaz searched for the source of this blue light as it dissipated. Her eyes, coming back to her, widened when she found it.

It came out of nowhere. Diaz increased power and tried to veer off. A dark mass rapidly rose from the land below them. It glowed softly as it closed the distance with the Blackhawk. It was a massive, circular object, covered in pulsing lights. It looked as big as a C17, one that was rocketing towards them.

Diaz wrestled the controls, veering hard to the right. But it wasn't enough, Diaz realized they were about to collide. Time seemed to slow as she watched the strange object fill her vision, bracing for impact the whole while as their interior was once again filled with blue.

The last thing Diaz remembered was the blinding light filling her vision, and overcoming her.

Now

Diaz watched her breath cloud in front of her, stunned as the memories returned to her in the darkness. The moon was eerily bright overhead.

Something was very, very wrong. Her mind raced as she tried to piece together what all had happened. She was sure that the Blackhawk had collided in midair with the aircraft (object?). What the hell was that thing? Where was her helicopter? And her crew? How the hell was she still alive and not canned lunchmeat scattered across an Afghan mountainside?

Regardless, Diaz needed to find the others, alive or not, no matter what. It was apparent she was on her own and in this hostile territory. She stood up and adjusted her NVGs on her helmet, next flipping the safety off on her handgun. She took out the GPS that she kept strapped to her flight vest and tried to orient herself. To her frustration, the electronic compass couldn't get a lock on anything. It just spun in circles.

She cursed the electronic device and, at the same time, she saw a white flash out of the corner of her eye. An owl sat perched on a neighboring boulder, much like a barn owl from back home. It stood tall and regal upon the stone. Through the darkness, two black eyes stared back at her. Diaz froze as she studied the owl. She was surprised; she didn't know owls lived in Afghanistan. They both remained motionless. The owl seemed regard her with curiosity and interest, then it spread its wings and silently leapt into the air.

As Diaz followed the owl through the white phosphor tubes of her NVGs, a rhythmic flashing light caught her eye as the owl flew into a cusp of trees ahead. Diaz stepped off, moving quickly towards the light, she knew that flashing anywhere. Diaz stayed low as she hustled through the brush into a clearing as the Blackhawk came into view.

In front of her lay her aircraft, its infrared strobe flashing in the night. The owl perched on the helicopter's tail as wind gently rotated its blades in a lazy circle.

It was as if her Blackhawk had been placed carefully, in this exact spot, in this remote wilderness. Making even less sense, it looked completely intact. Unharmed. Untouched. Not destroyed by an inflight crash. As Diaz approached, her pistol at the ready, she became more unsettled at this condition.

The owl once again leapt into the air and soon roosted among the trees. Diaz approached her aircraft, pistol up as she scanned left to right. She approached the open cabin door and carefully cleared it. Taliban could have beaten her to it, or maybe even left a trap. But the aircraft was clear, and as she looked around it everything seemed to be untouched and where it was supposed to be. Yet, there was no sign of her crew.

What she did find was one of the crew chief's weapons; an M4 with a magazine still loaded. Additionally, she found that the two M240 machine guns were still mounted. If the weapons were still here, then it was a safe bet the locals hadn't been here.

Diaz grabbed the M4. *Better safe than sorry,* she thought, sending a round home into the chamber.

She made her way to her seat up in the cockpit, hopping in and laying the M4 in the copilot seat. She ran some checks and everything seemed in order. But when she tried to start the aircraft, she was met with silence. She tried again and, again; silence.

"Fuck," she muttered out loud. Flying out of here wasn't an option.

She tried to boot up her Blue Force Tracker, but it wasn't drawing power either. She tried the radios to no avail, everything was dead. With no power, this aircraft was now a part of the mountain.

She reached into her gear and took out her personal radio for escape and evasions—perfect for such an occasion. She turned the power knob and prayed in the darkness that it would work, and to her relief the screen turned on with a soft beep.

Diaz keyed the mike as she glanced down at her GPS. "Mayday mayday, this is Clydesdale 66, we are Winchester at grid four two sierra x-ray golf eight five eight six one one nine one." She said it several times into the radio, praying that each time someone would hear her call. But each time she was met with silence.

"Fuck," she whispered. Diaz desperately hoped that whatever happened, at least the Blue Force Tracker, before it had died, had been able to transmit their last position.

Blue light suddenly lit up everything outside. Diaz strained her eyes. She struggled to look out there, half blind, as if on instinct trying to find the source of this pulsing light. It was so bright it almost burned, and Diaz's reflexively shut. After a time it dissipated, and when it did she noticed three figures now standing beside the aircraft.

Then the owl hooted.

Diaz reached for her M4 as she scrambled out of the cockpit. She wasn't about to be taken if she could help it. Diaz jumped behind one of the M240s switching the selector to fire.

"Halt, or I'll fire!" she cried.

The figures didn't move a muscle. She couldn't make out their details. The clouds must have moved in and her NVGs suddenly weren't as effective as they usually were.

Diaz remembered that the M240 had a PEQ15 on it; an infrared laser used to target anything unfortunate enough to shoot at them. It was infrared; her NVGs would pick up what it illuminated. She carefully moved the M240 to point directly at the chest of the middle figure. Its invisible beam then struck, revealing a man wearing an American uniform.

"Bazgew!" Diaz shouted, "Is that you?"

The figures remained motionless.

She moved the beam to the other two, revealing Chu and Hernandez. Both who, like Bazgew, still remained unresponsive. Diaz scooped up the M4 now, toggling on the attached PEQ15. With the rifle at the ready, she crept from the helicopter towards her crew, waving and saying their names.

Diaz crept closer; they stood like strange statues. She could see they all were staring straight ahead; wide-eyed and with faces like stone.

"Bazgew, Chu, Hernandez; are you ok? Can you hear me?" She took out a small flashlight and toggled on the IR to get a better look.

The three men remained still, gazing as if into some unseen abyss. Even through her NVGs, Diaz could see their eyes had a glazed look, like no one was home behind them.

The hairs on the back of her neck started to stand up. Diaz grabbed Bazgew's collar and violently shook him. "Bazgew, snap out of it!"

Her copilot suddenly came to with a gasp. Lieutenant Bazgew fell to his knees, almost dragging Diaz down with him. His breathed rapidly and shallow, now flailing in the dark.

"Calm the fuck down. It's me, Diaz!" she yelled.

"Diaz!? What the fuck?" Bazgew said as he started to come to his senses. Trying to catch his breath, "Where the fuck are we?" he said. "What happened?"

"I have no fucking idea. The last thing I remember was hitting something in the air."

Diaz herself tried to remember. She continued, "Next thing I knew I woke up on the ground next to the helicopter. I found you guys just standing here."

"My head is killing me." Bazgew put his hands to his ears. "What the fuck happened to—how are we not dead?"

"I have no idea what's going on. When I found you, it was like you were in a trance." Diaz responded before pausing, "like these two."

"Well, I don't remember shit." Bazgew said. "Are they... okay?"

Diaz looked hard at Chu and Hernandez. "I don't think they can hear us."

Diaz and Bazgew shook their fellow crew members, who also came to in a bewilderment of panic. The two pilots did their best to calm the crew chiefs, who barely held onto any semblance of composure. They too suffered from headaches and memory loss.

Diaz mustered her crew back into the Blackhawk, repeating her story again to Chu and Hernandez. Diaz watched the three begin the futile attempt to troubleshoot the helicopter. She once again tried to call over the emergency radio to anyone who may be listening…but static answered her back.

Hernandez slammed his fist on the door. "The bird is dead as fuck. I don't know what's wrong with it, but it's not gonna fly."

"This is bad, really bad." Bazgew said blankly, staring out into the darkness.

Diaz placed a hand on his shoulder. "We'll figure this out, someone is bound to notice eventually. I bet they already have."

Chu, who had walked to the tail to check a panel, suddenly shouted to the other three: "Ugh guys, come here and look up at the sky."

Diaz and the others walked to Chu and looked up into the darkness. At first, Diaz didn't know what to look for. Then she realized it. The stars. When she woke up the sky was clear, the starry sky in full glory. But now, they were gone. All gone. In their place was darkness, a true darkness devoid of anything. She'd first assumed it was the clouds rolling in, but now she felt the color drain from her face as she realized she'd been wrong.

Something was blocking the sky.

Diaz's heart began to beat faster. Above them was the perfect outline of a circle. An artificial pitch-black blotting out the stars on the other side. Something was looming up there. Despite the mountain cold, Diaz began to sweat.

It was *the* object.

"What the fuck…" one of her crew members started to say, but they didn't get to finish.

Because suddenly, that familiar blue light overwhelmed the flight crew. They shielded their eyes as they looked skyward, blinded.

Diaz began to shout to run to the helicopter, but her voice was drowned out by a mechanical humming that filled the air. Her crew members didn't need to be told to run for cover and were already moving. Diaz followed them. Rocks and pebbles began to rise around her. Her M4 was pulled from her hand. Then a peculiar feeling came over her, her movements became sluggish and delayed. She suddenly felt like she was moving underwater. At this newfound challenge, Diaz lost her footing. She began to fall forward, though, bracing for impact. But it never came.

She was floating in midair. Weightless. She struggled to right herself, but to no avail. She felt herself rising. Panicked, she looked around as her crew members shouted in astonishment. They too had begun to float skyward towards the source of the light, kicking and screaming. Even the Blackhawk was now off the ground, following the aircrew as they rose higher and higher.

Diaz suddenly found herself hanging limp as she stared skywards.

The last thing she saw was the haunting face on an owl, a face that welcomed her inside.

Twenty-Four Hours After the Crash

Chief Warrant Officer Percy Diaz strained her eyes against the bright white light above her. She sat in a room somewhere on Bagram, slumped in an uncomfortable metal chair and leaning on her elbows over a table. Across from her was a man wearing a sterilized MultiCam uniform, regarding her with a stone face. Diaz could tell he wasn't regular military. He was cold like the steel on a knife and his eyes cut right through her. While he didn't have a nametag, he introduced himself as "Barton."

Over the last several hours he had been her interrogator, continually questioning her about what she could remember.

She'd gone over the story a dozen times. "Again, that's all I remember," she'd said weakly.

He'd maybe scribble a note, or maybe he'd just stare.

"Where are the others?" she asked Barton.

"Irrelevant at the moment, Chief," Barton said plainly. "They are being debriefed just like you are. Again, what do you remember?" Barton paused, stone faced and waiting. She adverted his gaze; his eyes bore into her. When she didn't respond, he continued. "So, you have no memory of what happened? No memory of how you and your crew ended up in a field in Kandahar? How your aircraft was inexplicably deconstructed down to nuts and bolts and laid out neatly in a poppy field?"

Diaz just stared at him.

"Because I feel like we are missing some key details here, Chief. And it's imperative we get those details. Do you understand?"

Diaz struggled for answers, fought for the memories hidden away. But when she tried, the face of an owl stared back at her.

"I… I don't…"

Barton sighed as he got up from his chair. He walked over to the door and opened it, and he turned to her. "We've been talking for a few hours now," he said. I understand this has been a traumatic event for you, Chief. Take a break and get some fresh air. When you come back, we're going to continue." And a guard in a sterilized uniform appeared through the open doorway and greeted her, ushering her then away down a series of hallways.

Diaz followed the guard through the unknown facility, who soon brought her to an open-air courtyard. The buzz of helicopters in the distance droned over the night air.

The guard offered her a cigarette and coffee which she gladly accepted. She walked alone to a bench and sat down as he hung back at the door. Diaz lit the cigarette and took a drag with trembling hands, before washing it down with cheap government procured coffee. She grunted to herself. She never smoked before, but tonight seemed a good place to start.

Barton probably saw through her feint. Diaz remembered coming to in that field, and those helicopters that were thundering overhead. Her own helicopter had in fact been disassembled and neatly spread out. She remembered how soldiers in MOPP gear lifted her onto a stretcher and loaded her into an aircraft, whisking her away. Diaz remembered the medical examiners discussing the surgical scars that had appeared across her body, as well as whispering about the metallic object they pulled out of her.

The truth was, she didn't want to remember. But she most certainly did.

Diaz looked up and exhaled. She watched the smoke rise and dissipate into the cold, clear night. She stared into that masterpiece; a starry heaven painted across the sky. Beautiful and mysterious. In days past, she would have stared with wonder and excitement: curious of the vast expanse displaying itself each night.

As she stared into the cosmos, she shuddered under the gaze of countless eyes. Because she didn't feel that same sensation. Not anymore.

As Chief Warrant Officer Percy Diaz gazed, an owl hooted somewhere in the distance.

She felt fear.

THE TRANSCRIPT

The following is a transcript recording of an interrogation conducted by Master Sergeant Joseph Hassan on an unknown detainee known only as "The Detainee."

[Begin recording]

[There a door opening and bootsteps. The door closes and locks]

MSG Hassan: Ok recording is a go. Sound test. Test test test. Okay I read you loud and clear. Date is November 17, 2003.

[Shuffling of equipment and paper]

MSG Hassan: Ok recording in progress. For the record,

subject is an approximately thirty-year-old military-aged male. Of Muslim descent, potentially ethnic background points to Iraq or Iran although it's currently unknown. Subject has remained silent since capture and has resisted enhanced interrogation techniques. Subject was extremely violent and combative with guards and handlers, injuring several. He has been placed in restraints, which has reduced violent outbursts. However, he has still attempted to bite several personnel.

[MSG Hassan clears his throat]

MSG Hassan: Due to my ethnic and religious background, I have been brought in to attempt to connect with the subject to determine how he breached a secured facility. And more importantly why.

MSG Hassan: [In English] Lets remove that hood. Ah, there you go. [Switching to Arabic] As-salamu alaykum.

[A chair slides along the ground and creaks as MSG Hassan sits down]

Detainee: [In Arabic] Wa ʿalaykumu s-salam. [May peace be upon you]

[Detainee laughs heartily]

Detainee: I believe for the sake of the record we can use a common language your superiors can easily understand.

MSG Hassan: Oh. I see you can speak English very well...where did you learn? The UK? America?

Detainee: You'll find that I know a great many things,

language need not be an obstacle in our discussion. Although I see your superiors believe the commonality of our skin and language will create some familiarity between us.

MSG Hassan: I see. Well then what should I call you?

Detainee: Nothing. You can call me nothing but that which you already know me. I am one of many. Nameless.

MSG Hassan: Ok then, Nameless, then who are you?

Detainee: I already told you.

MSG Hassan: Where do you come from?

Detainee: You already know where I come from.

MSG Hassan: Do I? Because last I checked this is the first time you have decided to open your mouth to speak.

Detainee: Again, you know who, and what, I am.

MSG Hassan: That's not an answer. If you keep this up, we will go back to our methods from before.

Detainee: And that proved effective how?

MSG Hassan: Answer the question.

Detainee: [Sighs] I am from what you call the "Cradle of Civilization," or for you specifically, what your father Ahmed called the "Holy Land."

MSG Hassan: So, you're Arab?

Detainee: No.

MSG Hassan: Persian?

Detainee: [Chuckles] No.

MSG Hassan: Pakistani?

Detainee: Ha! [Snorts] The lines drawn on a map do not define me.

MSG Hassan: I know how combative you've been, that's why you're in these iron chains now. I saw how you fought the guards until the restraints were on. If you cooperate, we can talk about walking back some of our measures. The United States is open to rewarding those who cooperate with us.

Detainee: But you have nothing to offer me.

MSG Hassan: I can take you back to the dogs you know that right? I saw that the dogs seemed to break this stubborn façade of yours.

Detainee: [Shouts] No! [Clears throat] No. No dogs.

MSG Hassan: Ah, so not so unbreakable. Keep the shit up and I'll throw you to the wolves we have here. The dogs like new play toys.

Detainee: Fine.

MSG Hassan: So, you appear to be educated. You speak English better than me. Well-fed and healthy. No ordinary man could pull off what you did. Who do you work for?

Detainee: I have no master.

MSG Hassan: [Chuckles] ISI? Mossad? Quds Force? Hamas? Al Qaeda? Any of these ring a bell? Should I go on?

Detainee: I told you. I have no master.

MSG Hassan: You see, I highly doubt that.

Detainee: I would be lying if I gave you any other answer.

MSG Hassan: So answer this then, why were you found sitting cross-legged in a secure location deep within Fort Bragg?

Detainee: [Laughing] I take it Task Force Orange wasn't amused with that.

MSG Hassan: You see, the fact that you know that name proves you're full of shit.

Detainee: Oh?

MSG Hassan: Yes.

Detainee: I told you; I know all sorts of things.

MSG Hassan: You're not as clever as you think, we know there's a mole. Someone feeding you information. Helping you.

Detainee: Noooo, *tsk tsk tsk*, it's just me. [Laughing]

[A struggle is heard. Furniture is moved and there is a soft thud. Someone gasps in pain]

[A crackling is heard. A yelp of pain follows]

MSG Hassan: Are you ready to tell the truth now? This cattle prod has plenty of juice, and I have plenty of time.

Detainee: [Begins to laugh]

[Cracking is heard again and another yelp follows]

MSG Hassan: I'm tired of your fucking games. You understand English enough, so cut the shit and answer my questions.

Detainee: Ok, ok. I yield. I yield.

[Bootsteps and movement is heard]

MSG Hassan: We're going to try this again. Where are you from?

Detainee: I am from the place of your ancestors, Yusuf. Where your great-grandfather's grandfather walked the sands.

MSG Hassan: [Grunts] That's not my name.

Detainee: That's what your mother calls you.

MSG Hassan: Nice guess, but you're wrong.

Detainee: I know I'm right. Inaya calls you Yusuf. But Joseph you are because she didn't want her son to have a name so different from all the proper little American children.

[There is a long silence, approximately two minutes]

MSG Hassan: How did you breach Fort Bragg and gain access to Task Force Orange?

Detainee: Because I can go where I please. Borders, walls, fences, doors; these things mean nothing to me.

MSG Hassan: Answer the question.

Detainee: Because I can, Yusuf. [Growling] Because. I. will.

MSG Hassan: Who trained you?

Detainee: No one, all my skills are inherited.

MSG Hassan: What does that mean?

Detainee: Magic, Yusuf. Magic.

MSG Hassan: What did I say about these games?

Detainee: Concentrate, use that head of yours. Or have

you really forgotten the stories of your culture? The tales of your people?

MSG Hassan: What are you talking about?

Detainee: I am Jinn, Yusuf. Remember those stories your mother would tell you to keep you in line? Little stories to scare little Yusuf into obedience?

MSG Hassan: [Snorts] Fables. Ghost stories to scare children and again, you're full of shit.

Detainee: They're real. I'm real.

MSG Hassan: You've lost me and I'm not fucking around.

[Movement and electric crackling is heard]

Detainee: [Yelling] How about this Master Sergeant Joseph Hassan, US Army. Enlisted in 1985. Born at Bronx Children's hospital October 29, 1967. You wet the bed until you were eight. Have the scar across your face from when your father beat you, but you tell everyone it was from falling down the stairs. Your first kiss was Randi Jo Johnson freshman year of high school but you never told anyone how she tasted like cigarettes and bubblegum.

[An impact and screaming is heard. It sounds as if MSG Hassan strikes the detainee]

Detainee: [Screaming] Do I have your attention now!?

MSG Hassan: What the fuck is this? [Addresses someone else] Are you hearing this? Who the fuck is this?

Detainee: What's the matter? Shocked? I told you I know

a great many things.

MSG Hassan: We're done here.

Detainee: I breached Task Force Orange because I can. Because I could. So I could be here. In this room. To be heard…and you will hear.

[A hum is heard and several voices began to whisper. The detainee begins to chant in an unknown language. Analysts suggest that the detainee and the additional voices heard are speaking a potential ancient form of proto-Sumerian]

[Multiple voices begin to overlap with the detainee's chants]

Detainee: Are you listening? [It now sounds as if multiple voices are speaking at once with the detainee]

[Chains hit the floor]

Detainee: Your bonds mean nothing to us.

[Furniture is heard being thrown across the room]

MSG Hassan: What the fuck!

[Bootsteps are heard as well as pounding on a door]

MSG Hassan: Hey! Open the fucking door, it's locked! [Slamming is heard]

Detainee: I am here to bring a message. Not to you. To your superiors who will review the recording of this encounter.

[Multiple voices scream]

MSG Hassan: Let me go! Let me go!

Detainee: We are not your ally. We are not your enemy. We are beyond the world of men. We are nameless. We go where we choose.

[An explosion is heard as the door to the cell is breached]

Unknown: On the floor or we will shoot!

MSG Hassan: Help!

Detainee: The lands you occupy were never man's to claim. Let the wars of man continue once again, like they always do. Tread carefully in the Near East, for we are the true kings.

Unknown: Comply or we will shoot!

Detainee: This is not a warning. This is a threat.

[Several overlapping screams are heard as gunshots ring out before suddenly fading to silence]

Unknown: Holy shit! Where the fuck did they go!?

Unknown: Cut the recording! Cut the recording! We have a Code Black! Code Black!

[Recording abruptly ends]

The transcript appeared on "ANONLeaks" in 2017 and was subsequently deleted in 72 hours. MSG Hassan is officially listed as "Killed in Action on 13 January 2004 supporting Coalition operations as a part of Operation Iraqi Freedom."

MAN'S BEST FRIEND

A convoy of vehicles charged through the flowing traffic as Iraqi civilians lazily weaved in and out of the way. Twelve-gun trucks rumbled down the narrow roads under the hot sun, barely fitting on the roadway. Their gunners scanned the rooftops and traffic for threats, both in plain sight and any signs of hidden danger. The streets of Nasiriyah, Iraq were crowded with civilians going about their lives as best they could in. It had been over a year since the invasion and the battle for the city, but it still bore the scars from when Task Force Tarawa crushed the Iraqi Army in the early days of the war.

The city had been relatively calm since the Americans

stood up Combat Operations Base Adder. Until the war had returned, as the burgeoning insurgency had made its home in the city; with all manner of extremist, diehards, killers, and fiends aiming to carve out their own strongholds here. Now the Americans plunged into the city's depths, searching out the numerous cancerous cells; all threatening the coalition's peacekeeping efforts.

Gunner lifted her nose to the air. She lay on the bed of the transport at the feet of her handler, Specialist Tovar, as the vehicle bounced down the road. Even in the troop transport, her sense of smell revealed the world around her, even if she couldn't yet see it. She smelled everything, from the cologne of a passing Iraqi to the apprehension of her fellow soldiers.

Her ears perked when a soldier yelled over the roar of traffic and the groaning truck engine, "So are we seriously going after some serial killer?" Then that soldier spit into a bottle. Gunner twitched her nose at the wintergreen that wafted.

"Not a serial killer," another soldier replied, "some *haji* satanist fuck or something."

"Remember what the S2 said? The locals think he practices black magic, summons demons and shit."

Gunner's ears turned towards Spc Tovar, who was saying, "He's a cultist. Believes in some ancient religion. Some sick fuck who kidnaps and murders people to drink their blood."

"So...a *serial killer*, dumbass?" The soldier next to him gave Tovar a push on the shoulder.

Tovar just shrugged with a chuckle, "Sure. A serial killer."

"Fuck me, man. Did you ever expect to arrest a serial killer in a warzone?" The dipping soldier said as he spit once again into his bottle.

"Apparently the locals say he lives up in some old mansion, keeps all the windows boarded up and the house in the dark," another soldier piped up. "Likes to kill people with a machete."

"Great, we're dealing with an Iraqi Freddy Krueger."

"That's Jason, dipshit!"

The soldiers continued, back and forth, and Gunner selectively tuned them out to focus on the other sounds around her. She really only cared about what her handler said, and she looked up at him for any commands. Tovar just smiled and gave her the command for "at ease," which meant she could relax. He reached down and patted her head as she leaned into it. Gunner had quite a few handlers, but she had bonded better with Tovar than with the others and Tovar preferred working with her over the other dogs too.

Gunner was a three-year-old Belgian Malinois and had been in Iraq since the invasion; one of the first military working dogs in country. The soldiers had bestowed upon her the rank of "Sergeant," and she carried herself like a seasoned vet. Gunner was trained to find things: people, drugs, weapons, the occasional explosive device; and she was dammed good at it. She rarely lost a scent and had keener senses than the other dogs.

More importantly, she wasn't afraid of a fight. Unlike some of the others, she wasn't easily startled or frightened. Explosions and firefights didn't faze her. She had a reputation for keeping her calm under fire and was a favorite for missions that involved higher amounts of danger. The soldiers liked to talk about her "confirmed kill;" she charged a gunman that opened fire in a market, breaking free of her previous handler and diving through bullets to rip the gunman's throat open.

The troop transport began to slow before lurching to a stop as Gunner and the soldiers braced themselves. A speaker crackled to life as a voice announced they were to dismount.

Gunner's ears were up and she breathed in the scents of their stop. The same musty desert air she had grown accustomed too, trash, excrement, blood, and...something else? No, something new. Something that taunted her instincts. But she didn't have time to process it just yet.

The soldiers stood up and gathered their gear in the back of the transport. Another soldier quickly walked around back and opened the tailgate before hooking in a ladder for them to dismount. One by one, the soldiers climbed out. Tovar scurried down the ladder and signaled Gunner to come to him. Gunner walked to the edge and waited patiently as she panted in the hot air.

"Alright, stay Gunner, easy now." Tovar scooped her up and placed her on the ground. "That's a high jump, girl, got to watch those joints," Tovar said to her as he patted her head. "You're getting old, girl."

Gunner shook her body and stretched; her tactical vest felt heavy after sitting in the back of the truck. Tovar fished out a treat and offered it as she wagged her tail, she would never say no to a treat. Tovar then hooked on her leash and led her away, whistling a command. Gunner tensed her body and went on alert.

She took the chance to take in her surroundings. The trucks and soldiers were arrayed around a large house in an open area of the city. This area looked older compared to where she had been before, but many of the buildings smelled run down and abandoned. The soldiers pulled security around her, but as far as she could sense there weren't many civilians around. Like they were avoiding it. The air seemed off here, and it sat still and heavy in her lungs.

But her attention was soon brought to the large house that loomed over them all. At one point, this was a mansion of sorts, catering to a wealthy family before Saddam's rise to power. Now it was a decrepit thing, run down and in disrepair. The windows were boarded up and is seemed the only entrance was the front door which hung slightly ajar. Trash and refuse littered the courtyard, as well as bones of an unknown type scattered about.

"This place looks like a crackhouse," Tovar quipped.

Another soldier, the intel specialist attached for the mission, responded. "Heard that the owner was some Baathist bigshot under Saddam," he said, "part of the *Fedayeen*. Liked to torture people in the basement while his kids played upstairs. Supposedly he fell out of favor with Saddam after he started drinking blood and practicing black magic. The locals say that he sacrificed his family for some great power and the only reason he wasn't dragged through the streets was because we invaded that night."

Gunner huffed quietly as her eyes were locked on the door. A group of soldiers broke off to stack up on the house, Tovar and Gunner fell in behind them as part of the second group. A soldier cautiously opened the door, sweeping his rifle through the passageway as he entered. The others in the stack followed suit, carefully entering the dark confines of the house, rifles at the ready.

"Clear! Dog Up!" Tovar's radio barked to life.

"Alright, Gunner, let's move." Tovar said as she moved in synch with his steps. Her body was low and tense, ready to spring into action.

But as she passed through the threshold of the doorway, her hackles went up. Something was different about this place, something that triggered an alarm deep within her. The air seemed to crackle in here, buzz with some type of... force. This place was in full degradation and the smell of death permeated the air; not that sickly sweet smell of rotting flesh, but the smell of death itself.

Something wasn't right about this place; she was sure of that. Her canine ears could hear a strange heartbeat deep within this house and whispers that seemed to come from a deeper place within the void of darkness. She was overwhelmed with the unnaturalness, and she found herself freezing just feet inside the threshold.

Her lease went tight. She refused to take another step.

Tovar was jerked back by the dead weight on his hand. Unlike the others, he didn't jerk the leash in frustration. He sensed Gunner's apprehension and eased back towards her.

"Tovar, what the fuck is wrong with the dog?" A sergeant demanded.

"I don't know, sergeant. This isn't like her at all." Tovar knelt down.

"What's up, girl? Alert?" he queried Gunner.

Gunner looked him in the eyes and whimpered. Her fur was standing up as she tapped her paws on the ground, panting in nervousness.

"Sergeant, something's up. Gunner is bugging out—this isn't like her."

"I don't fucking care. Can the dog do the job?" the sergeant retorted. "We're after a fucking psycho Haji and I don't have time for a spooked dog. The 'terp said he's in here and is supposed to be a killer. I'm not here to take chances."

Gunner huffed again in displeasure, there was something wrong. Something unnatural. There was an energy that reverberated in the air that was only being felt by her. And it frightened her.

Tovar patted her head and looked in her eyes.

"Come on, girl, need you in the game. On me."

Gunner shook her head, pushing her fear to the back. Her handler was right, she needed to do what she was trained to do, what she was *bred* to do. She gave a huff.

"Atta girl, now come on. Seek, Gunner. Seek." Tovar looked up. "We're good, sergeant."

"Alright. Lead the way, Tovar," the sergeant said. "Let's find this fuck."

Gunner breathed in through her nose and listened. She could hear all the soldiers' heartbeats—and another heartbeat, coming deep from within the house. She smelled the unmistakable stench of another man. She walked forward and pulled Tovar after her.

The soldiers moved slowly. The walls were peeled and

the floors cracked as they walked down a hallway. It smelled of mold and rot, even he humans could smell it; the kind of stink found in places long forgotten. It was pitch black except for the light of the open doorway, and the soldiers soon used their flashlights on their helmets and rifles to see.

The dark didn't stop Gunner, in fact she could see better without the flashlights. She passed through a small hallway and another set of large wooden doors before stepping into the mansion's main foyer. Two large staircases spiraled opposite of each other to a landing.

Without warning, the doors behind them slammed shut.

"What the fuck?" a soldier shouted. "Who closed those doors?"

Two soldiers hustled back and tried to open them, soon resorting to using a halogen tool.

"The fucking door is jammed shut," one yelled. "We can't open them."

"All the windows are bricked up too," said the other. "No way we can knock that down."

The sergeant tried to use his radio to call the security detail outside. All that replied was static.

"I can't get through on the radio," he said. "Something is jamming the signal."

Gunner let out a low growl as her hackles rose once more.

"Stop!" the sergeant said suddenly. "Do you guys hear

that?"

Dozens of voices were whispering in the dark. Voices without character and identity. It sounded like they were conspiring amongst themselves, whispering in a strange language low enough so that their unexpected guests couldn't hear what they were saying. At once it sounded as if they reached an agreement and their tone changed to something more menacing as the voices began to chant a singular phrase. They began to grow in volume until their whispers were now shouts. The Americans used their flashlights, shining up and down the foyer but couldn't locate a thing. The voices seemed to be coming from every direction, as if materializing out of the air itself. Their flashlights soon began to flicker, casting shadows that seemed to move along the walls.

The whispers rose into a cacophony before silencing themselves abruptly.

"Hey," a soldier said, "what the fu—" all their lights went out at once. They were now in pitch blackness.

The soldiers tried in vain to get the lights working again. But, as they panicked, Gunner's eyes were locked ahead. Unlike her fellow soldiers, she could see just fine. And she tucked her tail between her legs.

Gunner watched a mass, darker than the darkness around it, rise up in front of them. The mass formed was twisting into a vaguely human shape. Gunner began to whine, knowing this thing wasn't natural and certainly wasn't human. The dark figure in front of them all was gangly and thin and taller than the soldiers. Its limbs were too long and its arms almost touched the floor. A long, skinny neck extended from its torso and was topped with a misshapen, oval head. It stood slack and slouched, observing the soldiers. Then it launching forward with startling speed.

Gunner gave out a yelp and relieved herself in fear as she backed away, tugging on Tovar who swung around. Gunner met his eyes in the dark and gave out a whine.

"Gunner, what the—what's wrong?" he said, staring down in the darkness towards the deadweight on the end of the leash.

But Gunner watched in horror as dozens of shadowy hands clawed at Tovar. Her handler couldn't even gasp in surprise as they covered his face and pulled his rifle away. Gunner's leash fell as he was enveloped by shadow and slammed to the floor. Before he could catch his breath, he was dragged away, up the stairs and at an awful speed; all by a mass of shadows, into the darkness.

As Tovar vanished away, the other soldiers' flashlights came back on. They started yelling in shock and surprise. Regaining their bearings, they soon realized that one of their number was missing. Gunner watched the soldiers while she shivered in fear.

"Where the fuck is Tovar!?" the sergeant shouted.

Someone stumbled to the ground in shock, grunting out a guttural "What the fuck!?"

"Gunner is still here sergeant!" another soldier yelled.

The whispers came back, growing louder in volume. But this time, it was no longer the indecipherable whispers as before. It was laughter. Eerie and taunting, from dozens of unseen mouths. Along the walls, shadowy figures materialized. Women. Children. Men.

"This is so fucked!"

Through the foul laughter, Gunner's keen ears picked up a noise. It was coming from deep within the house, a noise that cut through her fear, the distinct screams of a man. She heard his frantic heartbeat as he shrieked in terror.

But above her own terror, Gunner's training started to rage. Her fear began to melt away, slowly replaced by cold animal savagery. She had failed. Failed to protect her handler, her fellow soldier. She was going to do what she was bred to, what she was meant to.

Her mouth began to froth as the laughter echoed all around her. She breathed in the rancid, putrid stench of this evil place, finding a familiar scent deep within the house. Her mind was made up and her body became action. She snarled and bared her fangs in the face of the laughter. Gunner stepped forward, muscles and tissues firing as she then ran past the soldiers and up the stairs; bellowing a challenge with her bark.

"Gunner, what the fuck!" one of them yelled behind her.

"Holy fuck, Gunner's got a scent, get the fuck after her!" yelled the Sergeant as he sprinted up the stairs. The others soldiers followed, and the laughs grew louder.

Upstairs, Gunner turned towards a dark hallway. The terrified screams of Tovar echoed somewhere out of sight. She was faster and nimbler than the others. Locked onto his scent, she sprinted in the dark, barking with all her might so the others could follow. Shadowy figures reached out as she dodged and weaved, the voices attached to such groping began to shift from mocking laughter to furious screams. Gunner knew she was getting close.

She entered a large room. The walls were adorned with strange symbols. Bodies were scattered about the edges of the rooms in various stages of rot...throats slit and blood emptied. Gunner ignored the horror around her, instead fixing her eyes and snout on the center of the room.

Tovar laid on a stone alter. Four shadows held each of his limbs as he struggled against their strength. Something like a man stood over Tovar; emaciated and dreadful, holding a dagger in one hand and a rotting human heart in the other. A torn and tattered Iraqi officers uniform hung off his flesh like a robe. His eyes and mouth glowed with a hellish green light and he chanted in a human language she did not understand. His mouth agape, with rotting teeth filed down to points, consumed an ethereal mist that flowed out of Tovar's mouth. With eve moment Gunner could hear Tovar's heart beat slower and slower.

The strange man then snapped his glowing gaze to her, dropping the heart which fell with a sickening squelch. He pointed a long, bony finger towards her as he shrieked. Her fear began to well up again, but the killer inside her stifled it. Her hair stood and she bared her fangs, snarling a challenge in return; teeth like daggers and eyes sharpened to knives. The voices turned frantic and Gunner's ears rang with the volume of their screams. But she would not be deterred.

She moved with the speed of a predator. Adrenaline and killer instincts pumped through her blood. The dog stepped aside for the wolf buried deep within. Her claws sliced at the floors as she propelled herself over the alter, aiming for the man with murderous intent. The man's face grimaced with rage. The shadowy figures released Tovar as they tried to subdue Gunner. The man swung the knife, but while he may be a practitioner of the dark arts, he lacked the skill to kill something that fought back. He was too slow.

The voices now screamed in horror as he and Gunner collided. He fell back, striking the floor hard, the knife flying from his hand. He tried to shove and struggle against the dog, his unkempt hands grasping at her fur. Without hesitation, Gunner put her teeth to work. His flesh tore easily as she removed his windpipe and severed his artery with a crunch and a spray of blood. The man's eyes suddenly lost their glow as they widened. She could feel shadowy hands begin to grab her as she snapped her teeth back down on his throat. She thrashed as his blood splashed and his pathetic life gurgled out of him.

Then, all at once, the voices were gone and the shadows along with them. The strange man was dead and missing his throat. Gunner stood over her kill, and the wolf within her howled.

But the good dog soon returned. She turned her attention towards Tovar, who still lay on the alter pale and weak, seemingly sapped by the dark magic he had been subjected too . She jumped up and stood over him, licking his face, whining and crying as Tovar embraced her.

The others soon caught up, bathing the room in white light, staring in disbelief at Tovar and Gunner. They stared at the body on the floor and at the bloody dog that jumped all over their missing comrade. The soldiers all stared at each other next in disbelief over what just happened and the corpses that surrounded them. The sergeant's radio crackled to life. A loud thud indicated that the soldiers outside had finally managed to breach the doors.

"Hey, sergeant, looks like this is our Iraqi Freddy Krueger," one of the soldiers said, kicking the dead man with his boot. "Confirmed KIA."

Another soldier snapped a picture on a cheap digital camera.

The sergeant lit a cigarette and took a drag, staring at Tovar and Gunner. He exhaled and stared in disgust at the bodies lying all over the room.

He sighed, "They don't pay us enough to do this job."

LEGION OF THE DAMNED

PART I

First Lieutenant Frederick Rayburn wiped the rancid sweat from his eyes as he took a knee in the Afghan dust. The climb up the mountain had left him panting and his leg muscles burning and screaming as the lactic acid plagued them. He was exhausted, but his pride wouldn't let his men see that.

Rayburn gave a hand signal and command to his platoon, which was echoed by his squad leaders. They had come upon a dense area of trees; the concealment and shade was a welcome sight for the infantry platoon. The platoon spread out and pulled security, welcoming the tactical pause.

His platoon had been at it for hours, on patrol since the sun began to peak above the mountains. Doing what they did best: search and destroy.

He took a moment to catch his breath before reaching into his cargo pocket to grab a dirty and crumbled map. He unfurled it and checked his grid on his GPS, making marks on the paper with a pencil.

We're in the right spot, he thought.

He reached out and patted his radioman on the shoulder. The radioman unhooked a hand mic and passed it over. Rayburn then keyed the mic. He soon heard the familiar tone indicating that he was transmitting,

"Gator Six, this is Maniac Two Six."

A voice crackled on the secured frequency, "Maniac Two Six, this is Gator Six. Send it."

Rayburn could recognize the hardened voice of his company commander anywhere. Rayburn was a prior enlisted officer and former 11B-Infantryman, as was his company commander. Where they differed was that his company commander "went to the dark side" as a former First Sergeant. The man was intense and demanded excellence from his formation. Even as his commander was miles away at the patrol base, the platoon leader could feel his commanders' scrutinizing eyes.

"Gator Six," Rayburn said, "be advised, we are two klicks out from Objective Piedmont and at the release point."

The voice on the other end growled, "Roger, Maniac Two Six, be advised the Two has picked up radio chatter. Enemy contact should be expected. How copy?"

"Roger, Gator Six, enemy size and makeup?"

"Negative," his commander grunted back. "No intel on enemy forces."

"Maniac Two Six copies, Gator Six. Permission to proceed?"

"Affirmative. Good hunting, Gator Six, out."

The radio fell silent as Rayburn passed the hand mic back to his radioman. He then keyed his own internal radio, used for communication within the platoon, touching at the throat mic that was starting to chafe his neck.

"Gator Two Seven, this is Gator Six. We're clear to proceed."

The thick Puerto Rican accent of Sergeant First Class Vega came to life in his ear, "Roger, Six. Recommend we halt for thirty mikes, let the boys rest."

"Agreed, Seven. Put the platoon on fifty percent security. Thirty mikes, then we're on the move."

"Copy, Six."

Rayburn looked at the alarm on his wristwatch. *Thirty minutes*, he thought as he set the time.

He took the opportunity to drink from his camelback, the hot water soothing his dry mouth as he looked at the mountains that loomed and the ancient dust that blew in the apathetic wind. Rayburn was both captivated and intimidated by this beautiful place. The air reeked of untouched mystery and secrets.

His platoon was near the Wakhan Corridor, an isolated two hundred twenty-mile strip of land in northeastern Afghanistan. This place was considered the most isolated part of an already isolated country, it was practically untouched by any semblance of civilization. While the war had largely passed by this region, there were rumors that the Taliban sought to build a stronghold here. Second Platoon's patrol was part of a probe to gauge enemy activity in the corridor, the opening stages of a larger operation to sweep the area. Their company was tasked with establishing a patrol base near the mouth of the corridor and engage with the local population as a show of force in the region.

This area hosted some of the strangest people Rayburn had ever met. The people of Afghanistan were a strange lot but pleasant enough, when they weren't shooting at him. The people here in the Wakhan Corridor lived like it was still ancient times, with the occasional moped or decrepit rifle to break the façade. As revealed by Ali, the platoon's translator, most of the villages had never left the corridor nor had any idea the rest of the country existed. Let alone there was a war raging across it. The Taliban didn't ring a bell and a place like America was a myth. Ali stated that some families passed down tales of when their ancestors fought Alexander the Great. This land lived out of time, as if it was plucked from history itself. The air crackled with a strangeness that the men couldn't shake.

Because as Ali conveyed to Rayburn, this was a place where the people still warned of monsters and horrors hiding in the darkness. A place of demons and ghosts and terrible Jinn. The villagers' stories of ancient evils in the hills and valleys evoked some chuckles among the members of the platoon, a vain attempt to downplay stories designed to scare children into submission as some would claim. The people said so with such a straight face that it was hard to scoff at such a thought. To them, it wasn't some story passed down through generations. It was fact.

Upon completion of their very first patrol, Ali pulled the lieutenant aside and conveyed to Rayburn that these people were serious, and that he personally believed them.

"This place isn't like the rest of Afghanistan," Ali nervously told Rayburn. "The villagers are saying there are demons in the valleys and have taken many lives. They warned me that if we're not careful, they will kill us next."

Rayburn didn't believe in that backwater bullshit. "Nothing more than a ghost story told to keep people in line," he reassured Ali. "Probably some guys killing off wayward souls."

However, seven months of Afghanistan could make even the biggest skeptic superstitious. Rayburn and his soldiers had seen plenty of strange and horrible things in country, things that made them doubt everything. While he would never say it out loud, Rayburn had grown to take those warnings to heart.

The platoon was set to infiltrate an unnamed valley ahead of them, Objective Piedmont. Intel alleged that there was a system of caves in the mountains around the valley, which coupled with the close proximity to the border, fit the Taliban's preference. Their mission was to establish an observation post in the unnamed valley before them. It was avoided by the locals, as it was known as an "evil place" where people never returned from. However, the locals had insinuated that they had seen a large group of armed men moving into the valley some days prior. The Americans gathered that this could have been the Taliban they were after; scouting a potential stronghold in the region with local superstition keeping interlopers out.

Rayburn said a silent prayer. Even though he was used to the infantry life and being "alone and unafraid" on mission, he wasn't a fan of being this far away from support. If the Taliban discovered the American's were here, it was doubtful they would sulk away from a fight. Intel couldn't put a number on the size of the force that was reported entering the valley, only that it could be comparable to a "platoon-sized element." But with night inevitably closing in, his platoon needed to find a suitable hide to establish their observation post, rather than be caught moving around under the stars.

Rayburn's wrist was vibrating. It was time to move out. He reached for his throat mic and transmitted across his platoon, "Seven, this is Six, time to charlie mike." And with that, the platoon was up and moving.

They didn't have to march long before the opening to the valley between two cliffs loomed. It was narrow; just wide enough for men on foot and pack animals. It was hidden from view by a green wall of trees, which the platoon moved through cautiously, and while the trees offered a welcomed respite from the sun they also offered plenty of hiding places. This piece of terrain before the valley was a natural chokepoint and if the Taliban had recognized this, it was a perfect ambush point. Rayburn reached for his radioman's mic. Once he keyed it, static exploded through the speaker. He tried to transmit again, same result. He spoke into the static and waited for a reply. Nothing.

"What's up, sir? No comms?" said SFC Vega as he came running up.

Vega began to troubleshoot the radio, fiddling with the interface. He too received nothing but static.

"Mountains might be blocking the signal, sir," Vega said to the platoon leader.

"I'm not a fan of continuing without comms," Rayburn said.

"I feel you, but we should keep moving and find some higher ground; we're too exposed here to be halting." He relaxed slightly, as his eyes narrowed, "But it's your call, LT."

This was one of Rayburn's least favorite moments being a platoon leader, making a choice that had consequences for everyone if he was wrong. He took a fleeting moment to make a decision.

"Agreed, let's keep moving," Rayburn said. Like it or not, Vega was right.

The platoon continued into the valley in two columns. They followed a dried-up creek bed that created a natural trail. There were signs that someone had come down here recently, discarded trash and footprints were evident on the trail. As they entered the valley, they became surrounded on all sides by towering mountains. Their peaks loomed like the jagged teeth of a dead titan, and as they walked, Rayburn noticed that the air here was still, eerily still. It was quiet, even for a place so remote, and the only sounds at the moment were the bootsteps of his men.

The valley was dominated by a heavy pine forest, deep and dark, like something from a fairytale. Boulders and mossy stones littered the ground, as well as the ruins of some long-forgotten stone structure. There was a small river flowing nearby and rolling hills covered in lichen. This place seemed bigger than the valley depicted on the map, it looked nothing like Rayburn had expected, or had ever seen. Alarms started going off in his head—could they be lost? He gave a command to halt, and as they pulled security he pulled out his map and GPS. He studied the valley, trying to interpolate their position by terrain association. But he found that the map wasn't matching what he was seeing. When he tried to pull a grid off the device, he was shocked to find that it couldn't get a satellite. He shut off the device and tried to turn it back on, and after a few moments "No satellites found" flashed on the screen. He took out his compass, but it began to spin in circles like a broken record.

Before Rayburn could call Vega, the platoon's pointman yelled out that he had found something. A few of the men broke off and rushed to the front. Rayburn keyed his mic, "Point, this is Six. What's up?"

His radio crackled and the soldier called back, "Found a couple of bodies, military-aged males. Might be our guys, but…you'll want to see this for yourself, Six."

Rayburn scratched his head. "Seven, this is Six…I'm headed to the front of the formation."

"Six, this is Seven," SFC Vega responded. "I'm already here…Yeah, you're going to want to see this."

Rayburn trotted up to stand with his platoon sergeant. His eyes grew wide and his stomach began to do turns. He stood silently next to Vega at a loss for words.

Before them lay several Afghan males, or what was left

of them. Bodies lay scattered on the trail in various forms of grotesque dismemberment. Limbs lay away from bodies and guts were spilled out into the dirt. Rayburn had seen what modern firepower did to a human body, but this didn't look like that. Whatever had happened to these men, they didn't die well.

"Looks like we found our Taliban...," Vega said to his platoon leader. "I don't like this." He turned to bark orders at the squad leaders to pull security.

Rayburn approached two soldiers closest the scene. He then bent down at a body while the two started snapping pictures for an after-action report. Rayburn looked into what used to be a chest cavity. Except now it was an empty space: ribs cracked open and organs scooped out. All that remained was some shredded intestine. He picked up an off-white piece of material, only to realize that it was the remains of someone's rib. Whatever did this, it seemed to take the time to lick it clean and suck out the marrow. Rayburn tossed the bone away in disgust. Worse, the head to the body was gone; ripped away like a grape on the vine, and the rest of the body looked like it had been hacked at with knives. It looked like the aftermath of a predator attack, like these men had been torn limb from limb in an animal's frenzy. As he bent down to observe more bodies, it dawned on him that this shouldn't be possible. The only animals he knew that lived in Afghanistan big enough to do this were snow leopards and the rare hyena. But those preferred to avoid humans or hunt alone. Rayburn found it highly unlikely. *So then what the hell had happened?*

"Hey, we got a live one here!" shouted a soldier.

Rayburn shuffled over to where his two guys now stood over a new body. What was left of a man wiggled and coughed. Rayburn felt the bile rise in his throat and he felt himself recoil in horror. The man was missing every arm and leg. Large gashes covered his face, slashes that went around his eye sockets which now were both gaping and empty. How this man was alive was a mystery to Rayburn. He couldn't deny the cruelness of the violence inflicted on this man...and deep within his soul he knew something had done this because it had enjoyed it.

"Holy fuck, that's fuckin' fucked up, man. What the fuck," one of the soldiers stammered. "This is beyond fucked."

"Shut up—he's trying to say something," the other soldier said, pushing him aside. "We need Ali and a medic up here!"

Rayburn just stared, the body wiggling like a worm in the blood and dirt. He appreciated the humanity of calling for a medic, but this man was dead. He turned to watch the medic and Ali approach. The medic took one look at the scene and vomited onto the ground.

"Ali, get over here," Rayburn demanded. "What is he

saying?" Rayburn watched the terrified interpreter; how the color was draining from his face.

"Ali, wake the fuck up!" Rayburn shouted, his voice cracking from his own fear.

Ali hustled over, clumsily falling to his knees. He gulped and leaned his ear to the dying man. He winced and looked up at Rayburn, confused looking, before speaking slowly as the brown of his face drained completely. "He's saying something about demons. Demons, demons, demons, over and over again."

"What do you mean demo..." Rayburn started to say. But before he could finish, the doomed man at his feet died with the sound of a wet death rattle.

"Poor fucker," a soldier remarked.

Rayburn turned around to see Vega marching up to him, "Sir, we need to leave—now."

The lieutenant took a reluctant step backward before composing himself. "Our mission is to recon this area and set up an observation post. I don't know what this is about, but we can't let it scare us."

SFC Vega's face turned to stone. They stared at the other without a word until, at last, the platoon sergeant said calmly, "We've done our recon, sir. We should pullout and report this higher. Something is wrong here. I've tried calling back. Nothing. Without comms we're on our own right now." The usually stoic Vega was cracking and Rayburn could see it replicating in the faces of his soldiers.

"It's getting dark," continued Vega. "This is not the place to get caught with no comms and no support.

Rayburn thought it over. Vega was spooked. But, to his point, something was wrong and without comms they were on their own. If what was left of the Taliban or whatever did this decided to confront them, having no way to call for help meant none of them were getting out of here alive.

"Alright, let's egress out of the valley. We'll set up an observation post at the mouth and contact the rest of the company. Get the platoon on their feet."

With that Vega was in motion, getting the platoon organized to move. Rayburn turned to look over the bodies once again. *What happened here?* He gripped his M4 tighter. It was around then when something caught his eye, movement among some rocks in the distance. For a second, he swore he saw a dark shape scurry over them before darting from view. He suddenly had the distinct feeling that he was being watched. He raised his M4 and scanned the terrain. *Just my nerves*, he told himself.

Rayburn turned to join his platoon and they began moving swiftly back the way they came. He followed up at the rear, partly because the platoon started without him and partly because he wanted to make sure no one got left behind. Vega, eager to leave, took point with the map as they followed their footprints back to the pass. Rayburn couldn't shake that feeling: he was being watched. He kept glancing behind him, seeing if they were being followed. The men were jumpy, too. They gripped their weapons as if marching into a shoot house. The discovery of the bodies was enough, but Vega's demeanor only served to shake harder their nerves.

The platoon came to an abrupt halt. Rayburn looked over his men's heads and his blood ran cold as he saw what the cause for the stop was. The pass was gone. He looked around the sheer cliff face before them. The pass to the valley should be right here. But it wasn't. It was impossible. Yet, as he continued to scrutinize their surroundings, everything seemed different from when they had entered the valley. In front of them was exactly where they had come from. He could see their footprints. But now a massive cliff blocked their gone mountain pass. Rayburn ran to the front of the formation as Vega and several other soldiers spread out along the cliff face, searching in vain for a way through. He approached and placed a hand on the wall, it didn't seem real and yet here it was.

Vega came up to him with a map in one hand, GPS in the other. "It doesn't make sense. No fucking sense," he muttered. He then turned to the radioman, "Try again, call back to them."

The radioman soon shouted back, "No response, sergeant!"

Vega stammered to Rayburn, "It doesn't make any sense." Vega stormed off to retrace their steps, looking at the map in shock.

"It doesn't," Rayburn said, further examining the cliff. But before he could examine any further, his hair suddenly stood on end as his brain blared a klaxon that bounced off his skull. Screams reverberated off the canyon walls imprisoning his platoon. A wet, terrible screech that was so unlike anything Rayburn had ever heard. The scream began to fade, and as it did a chorus of other throats bellowed in response from the dark forest behind the platoon. All around him, his soldiers gripped their weapons; uncertain with fear, stepping closer and closer together with their backs against the cliff face.

Vega turned to say something, but his shout was stifled as something pierced through his neck. *An arrow.*

Vega clutched at his throat as he crumpled to the ground, scarlet blood gushing from his severed artery. Rayburn lunged for his platoon sergeant as blood splattered on his body armor. He tried to stop the bleeding with his hands as he screamed "Medic!" and desperately reached for the Vega's IFAK.

But, in the end, there was nothing Rayburn could do. Vega gurgled his final breaths as Rayburn looked up in horror to see the medic now take an arrow to the chest, sending him backwards. He scrambled away behind a boulder; the Kevlar plate of his vest having done its job.

"Contact front!" some soldier shouted. "They're coming out of the wood line!"

Rayburn stood, stunned, staring at Vega. Someone yelled "Open fire!" and the sharp clacks of a platoon's worth of M4s came to life as figures closed in. A burst from a M249 brought Rayburn back to reality, and he raised his own weapon.

Dozens of strange and grotesque figures rushed towards his platoon, while several more shot their arrows. Some ran on two feet, others galloped on all fours like animals, blending the line between beast and man. Screams that promised violence and death pierced the air. Rayburn shouldered his rifle, staring through his ACOG at the forms rushing towards him, and what he saw terrified him. Whatever was barreling towards him wasn't human. Some ancestral memory fired off in terror in the depths of Rayburn's brain. It screamed in recognition and Rayburn realized he was staring at something unnatural, *an aberration*. A face stared back at him as a mouth full of fangs screamed for his death. Like something ripped from some biblical painting, what he could only call a demon bared down on him. Its form was nothing more than a twisted mockery of man: reddish skin glistening, stretched taught over an emaciated body. Broken horns adorned its elongated head and scars crisscrossed its body. Clawed hands clutched both a rusty sword and a spear. Yellow eyes fired pure malice into Rayburn's eyes as he watched a purple tongue snake around dagger-like teeth.

Rayburn's placed the red reticle of his ACOG on the chest of the demon and he squeezed the trigger. His M4 pumped three rounds into the thing, and he watched rust-colored blood spray free. The demon stumbled onto its knees. It quickly regained its footing and continued its charge with a renewed rage. Rayburn exhaled and pumped two more rounds through the demon's skull; disintegrating half its face. The demon dropped its weapons then as it folded in half, slamming into the ground and skidding to a halt. As it twitched in the dirt, more descended from the hills; besieging the platoon, closing in for the kill.

Arrows and rocks rained down. The platoon tried to dodge and shoot. "Fire at will!" Rayburn screamed as he dropped to a knee, taking aim at the archers. He calmed himself, countless hours behind the gun began to pay off. Each figure he sighted in on was dropped with headshots. Rayburn burned through his magazine before he slammed in another, he and his M4 killing several more archers after. As the last one he saw fell back with a mouthful of 5.56mm, Rayburn took a look around.

The horde had encircled the platoon, cutting off all avenues of escape. With their backs against the wall, the soldiers were still firing. Demons sidestepped and scrambled past their dead. They soon reached their prey, falling on their victims with a violent fury, overwhelming several of his men.

Rayburn watched as Ali stood his ground, firing an M9 pistol in a futile effort as a demon bore down on him. The rounds blossomed on the demon's flesh, but its yellow eyes were locked on the kill. Wrapping a clawed hand around Ali's neck, its strength betraying its emaciated form, it lifted him off the ground with one hand. It screamed as it slammed the doomed man's body over and over. There was a sickening crunch Rayburn could hear over the gunfire as Ali's skull cracked like an egg. The demon bent over and scooped the man's brains off the ground. Rayburn fire three rounds into that creature, cutting its celebration short, avenging Ali. He pulled two grenades from his kit next, pulling the pins and throwing them towards the growing mass of bodies. The grenades landed in the demon's midst as they ran oblivious. Rayburn hit the deck as twin "thumps" sent shrapnel flying, dismembering, and scattering several enemy. It made the others stumble back in surprise. Rayburn took the opportunity.

"Machine gunners on me!" he cried, waving them towards him. "Get those fucking guns up!—Fall back behind the 240s!" he screamed to the rest of the platoon, many of whom repeated his command. "Form a firing line!"

His men fell back behind him, up against the cliff as the

M240s came to life. The machine guns sent a hail of 7.62 in a thunderous roar, ripping into the twisted bodies that bore down on them. The rest of the platoon followed suit as a concentrated wall of fire erupted. Some men lobbed grenades and fired their underslung grenade launchers, scattering and tearing the demons apart.

Over the staccato of the Americans weapons, Rayburn began to hear the distinct *clacks* of AK-47s. Several figures rose up on a hill to his right, firing into the wave of demons and throwing their own grenades. He saw two figures crouch, and the distinct whoosh of two RPG-7s fired at once, the explosions adding to their firepower. This new opponent was enough to surprise the demons, who were cut down en masse. The horde began to break apart and scatter back into the hillside under the combined fire of both parties.

"Cease fire! Cease Fire!" Rayburn shouted as he watched the last demon gunned down, abandoned by its brethren.

The figures up above began to approach. More than a dozen crested the hill and moved swiftly towards the platoon. Rayburn stepped forward and held his rifle up at the figures. He wasn't sure if they were friend or foe, but he wasn't about to risk his life or his men's after what had just happened.

"Halt. Coalition forces! Halt or I will fire on you!" he shouted holding his rifle in one hand and trying to wave off the figures with the other. They were men. Strange men. One of them then stepped closer, surveying the carnage before looking up at Rayburn.

He said, "Я не говорю по-английски, может кто-нибудь привести британского ублюдка?"

PART II

Rayburn's eyes widened—both in surprise and in recognition. Straight from a history book, the men in front of him, did in fact, resemble the Russians who invaded Afghanistan. They wore tattered uniforms of splotchy green and brown, but with blue and white undershirts. The blue beret on the man who spoke gave them away as paratroopers of the VDV. Rayburn counted: fourteen in all, each one of them clutching Soviet bloc weapons. Rayburn spied the RPG that had fired just moments ago, as well as a Dragunov sniper rifle.

The man in the blue beret studied him. His eyes rested on Rayburn's right shoulder. He turned to his squamates, and spurted out in Russian, "Похоже, американцы решили вторгнуться в эту богом забытую страну. Думаешь, они понимают, в каком аду они оказались?" Rayburn had no idea what he just said, but the other Russians began to murmur amongst themselves.

The man in the blue beret turned his attention back to Rayburn with an amused look on his face, "эй, американец, ты выглядишь так же, как тот американец, которого я помню. скажите мне, мы выиграли войну в Афганистане? или мы с тобой сейчас ссоримся? Не то чтобы это имело большое значение."

Rayburn lowered his rifle slightly as he stared dumbfounded. His men around him glanced at one another nervously as they too struggled to comprehend what the Russian said. The Russian rolled his eyes. He spoke in a comically thick accent, as he pointed with a free finger at himself, "My English. Shit."

Just then a man approached the group, as a loud cockney voice announced, "Oi—what's all this then? Lower your weapons friends, there's no need for that here."

A man in a British redcoat jogged up to them. His uniform was distinct as it was tattered, too old to make sense; complete with a saber that dangled from his hip. But the Brit held his own AK-47. He halted in front of Rayburn's platoon, sizing them up with the sharp eyes of a professional. He turned his attention to Rayburn and rendered a quick salute. "Major Benedict Masterson of Her Majesty's 43rd Regiment of Foot. At your service."

The man held his salute. Rayburn looked around, unsure of what to do next. Things just kept getting weirder. He decided to return the salute. "First Lieutenant Fredrick Rayburn," he said, awkwardly. "1st Platoon, Fox Company, 423rd Infantry Regiment."

Major Masterson smiled. "You'll have to forgive our comrades here. Leytenant Vortesky's English and my Russian are both quite shit. Our mutual language lessons are ongoing."

Rayburn eyed the major with suspicion, his eyes glancing between the Brit and the Russians. He looked behind him at the faces of his own men; those who had survived the battle. He took inventory of the survivors, thirty-two of the platoon's original forty-seven were still standing. Vega, Ali, and the rest lay dead in the dirt. Each of the survivors wore uncertainty and grim dread on their face. They were neck deep in whatever horror movie they had found themselves in.

Rayburn turned back to the major. "We're not going anywhere until you explain to me what the fuck is going on."

The major looked beyond the cliffs at the fading light of a dying sun. "I'm sure you have plenty of questions, Lieutenant, and I assuredly will attempt to answer them. But at the moment we are losing daylight and we do not want to be caught outside in the dark here…believe me."

The major's cheerful face suddenly hardened, "And if you don't want to die like the others," he motioned to Rayburn's slain men, "you'll follow."

Rayburn stared into the major's eyes and then into the Russians'. He could feel his heartbeat with fear, but they needed to find someplace defensible. He sighed, "Alright, we'll follow."

The major nodded, "Good," he said, "we will take you to the fort." He pointed down again at the bodies. " Your dead will have to stay here, they'll only slow us down." Rayburn started to object; he wouldn't leave the dead here to rot. But the major held up his hand. "They'll slow us down, and the more we daddle out here, *our* enemy will attack."

Rayburn stared at the major before reluctantly walking to one of the dead, he recognized the dead man as a young private from Minnesota. He stared for a moment before bending down and grasping at the dog tags covered in blood in the ruins of his neck. He pulled them off, silent in thought as stared at them. He bounced the bloody tags in his hand before shoving them into a cargo pocket on his trousers. He stared at the young soldier, thinking about the insanity of what occurred. He heard footsteps in the dirt behind him as the major came to stand next to him. As if reading Rayburn's mind he said, "Lieutenant, I know. Trust me, I know. The bones of my battalion litter this entire valley."

He placed a hand on Rayburn's shoulder, "I'd recommend grabbing whatever you need or want off of them. They'll buy us more time as a distraction…there won't be much left come morning."

The Major walked away from the Americans with his rifle slung across his back, tapping his saber with the tips of his fingers. He stopped and turned to Rayburn as if remembering something. "Things get a lot easier in the morning. I'll explain and answer all the questions you have at the fort." He glanced down at a pocket watch he pulled from his coat, "I'll give you ten minutes before we march."

The platoon quickly gathered the remaining dog tags, along with weapons, ammo, food, water; the supplies being dispersed just as quickly amongst them. There was some initial protest about leaving their dead, but ultimately the men understood.

Rayburn squatted down next to Vega. He had pulled out the arrows and at least crossed his arms. He said a silent goodbye before looking down at his friend one last time. He stared at the bodies of Ali and the others savagely killed by the demons. He felt his stomach knot up in anger and sadness. But he swallowed it deep, for now he had to keep the rest of his men alive. Standing up, he rallied the platoon behind him and now they all fell in behind the major, who took the lead with his Russian escorts.

They quick marched. They moved silently and with a quicker determination. The open hills and sparse vegetation of the cliffs gave way to a thick forest of pines. They moved along a meager river with their rifles up; the sun was going down and Rayburn could hear inhuman screams in the distance which gave way to an opera of bellows spread out in the distance, like packs of wolves getting ready for the hunt. It gave the otherwise quiet air, a chilling discomfort.

The group followed the river to a clearing in the trees. There in the middle, on a small hill, were stone walls and an ancient array of battlements. The major slowed his pace and then they all stopped. There was a mote dug around the walls, filled with a dark water that flowed into the river which appeared to pour out of several cuts along the wall. There was a stone bridge that led up a set of large, reinforced wooden doors.

Rayburn could still hear the bellowing in the distance. He signaled his men to cover the rear.

"Eh, Sarbaz," Major Masterson yelled, "open up! We've returned!"

After a moment, the doors creaked open. Several men rushed out wielding what Rayburn recognized as PKM machine guns. He noticed they were also Russians; paratroopers that looked more at home in the 1980s than current times. They ushered the group inside as they covered them, before slowly backpedaling past the doors. The *Kapitan* and his men then turned to cover the entrance with as the doors creaked shut.

Once done, the Russians dispersed into the courtyard. Only the man with the Dragunov remained behind. He climbed a ladder and took his place in a sniper's nest; peering out across the mote. The major approached what appeared to be a lone Afghan, who wore an ancient style of robes and leather holsters. This local had a long beard, with golden beads braided in and was a mountain of a man, standing at least half a head over the average soldier. He carried a rifle across his back and a sword on his hip, much like Major Masterson, who he then embraced in a bear hug.

"I am happy to see you alive ســور کــوټ," the Afghan said, slapping the Englishman on the back. "I was afraid I was going to have to fish you out of the fountain!"

"Ah, well, Sarbaz, can't get too lucky, I guess," the major said cheerfully. He then motioned to Rayburn and his men, "I've found the newcomers."

Sarbaz looked the Americans over, "Such strange newcomers, indeed. I wonder what kings these men belong to. Come, we have much to discuss."

Sarbaz and the major ushered the Americans to follow. The sky was getting darker and Rayburn watched men begin to man the walls and light torches to fend off the night. As he looked around, he saw Russians who were dressed just like the ones who'd saved him, men who looked similar to Sarbaz, and now a few more British redcoats. But he soon also saw men adorned in strange armor, wielding massive spears and swords. *Greeks?* And there were lumbering men adorned in gold and fur, walking to and fro, carrying large bows and swords of a different make. *Are these guys Mongol warriors?* Other warriors manned this fort; warriors whose origin Rayburn could not even guess. Rayburn and his soldiers then passed a figure hunched over fire, draped in furs. The man lifted his sloping forehead to look them over, holding all the while a heavy stone club.

Rayburn questioned if he had died and entered some fucked up Valhalla—*or is this the plot point in one of my dad's science fiction books I used to read back home?*

They soon passed a group of Afghan men who looked all too familiar to Rayburn. Their white Servis Cheetahs shoes and CHICOM chest rigs were a dead giveaway. They eyed the Americans with an uncertain intensity as they sat around a steaming pot of tea.

The major turned to Rayburn, shaking his head. "Newcomers just like yourself. Arrived a few months ago. Found them near the caves north of here, crazy bastards. Came in with a group of fifty or so, only ten survived. That group you found was unlucky enough to come looking for them."

Rayburn stopped and stared at the eldest of that group, a man whose dark eyes now bore holes into his own. The Taliban fighter sprang up, as did all the rest; all holding their AKs. Rayburn readied his rifle as the rest of the platoon followed suit. He gripped his weapon tight as he felt himself break out in a cold sweat as his heart began to pound. The Taliban stepped closer. A standoff between the two groups quietly burned in intense silence.

Sarbaz suddenly stepped between the groups with his

hands up, as if to part them. "No fighting," he said softly, but with authority, and in both English and Pashtun. "Whatever you were before, we are all corpses in the same grave now."

"Indeed," The major chimed in, stepping between the groups, talking in both Pashtun and English as well. "Sarbaz and I were once enemies." He motioned to Sarbaz, and then he chuckled. "In fact, if it wasn't for chasing this bastard, I wouldn't have ended up here."

"You could have let me escape my old foe," Sarbaz shrugged, laughing. "You chased me into this damned valley. This is your fault, not mine."

"Ha! Cheeky bastard. Being trapped in hell for over one hundred years will soften any hatred." The Major laughed, "If you want to survive, Lieutenant, you'll learn we're all a part of the legion of the dammed now!"

Sarbaz translated the major's words to the Taliban, emphasizing, "Because if there are any problems, you can wallow in them on your own outside these walls," adding, "before we were trapped in this hell, I was sworn to kill the major here. In fact," he laughed, "I almost succeeded!"

Major Masterson slapped his shoulder. "Well, luckily for both of us, you prove to be better with a sword than a rifle."

The Taliban and Americans both began to lower their weapons. The elder eyed Sarbaz, then Rayburn.

Slowly, the Taliban leader raised his hand: an outstretched parley. In a heavily accented voice, he said one word: "Peace."

Rayburn looked at his outstretched hand and then into the man's eyes. The eyes of his once enemy. The eyes of a man who looked like all the others that had tried to kill Rayburn and his soldiers. And had succeeded, as he painfully remembered. There was a hate that boiled in Rayburn's stomach, the same hate he was sure that still boiled somewhere in the Taliban's. But after what had transpired today, the major had a point. He preferred to live through this and not take his chances outside the walls of the fort.

He held out his hand, shaking the Taliban's. "Peace," he said plainly. "I am Rayburn."

"Peace," the Taliban leader said. "Mustafa."

"Well then," Major Masterson piped, "now that we are all tickled and made up, follow us." The major stepped off with Sarbaz.

They led the Americans deeper into the fort, to a large hut along a wall. "You gentlemen will sleep here tonight." He motioned for Rayburn and his men to enter.

Rayburn started to protest, "We're not doing a goddamn thing until you explain to us what the fuck is actually happening here."

The major cut him off. "Don't argue, Lieutenant. Your men need their rest. And you need not worry about our demonic foe on the outside, they avoid this place…

"I'm getting tired of this fucking shit." Rayburn interrupted.

The major's eyes hardened and Rayburn felt himself recoil slightly. The major started to say something, but he stopped himself, looking at Sarbaz and back at the Americans. "Things will get easier in the morning. Trust me. You don't rally have a choice not to"

Rayburn and his platoon reluctantly entered the hut. Still unsure of the easy peace made between them and the Taliban, he organized a watch rotation. Four men would be up at all times through the night. Better safe than sorry.

And he didn't shut his eyes much, nor did his platoon. The insanity of what had occurred threatened to tear them apart. The howling in the distance reminded him that the situation was very much real. Rayburn eventually drifted off into some semblance of sleep; the leering face of a demon haunting his dreams.

PART III

Rayburn awoke the next morning with a start. His night was without peace, haunted by horrors both man and not. The sun was rising over the mountain peaks. A bird tweeted outside the tent, oblivious to the hell that it was trapped in. Someone stirred him with a nudge of a boot.

"Hey, sir," a soldier on watch said. "That British guy is

headed this way."

Rayburn got up, wiping the exhaustion from his face. He put his plate carrier on and fetched his rifle before walking outside the hut as Major Masterson approached. He stood at the doorway as the cheeky Brit cheerfully shouted, "Good morning!"

Rayburn walked out to him and replied, "Good morning. I think it's time we talked."

The major nodded, "Agreed, Lieutenant. In the meantime, your men can head to the canteen."

Rayburn shook his head, "No, we're gonna stay here. At least until you answer my questions."

"Very well then, whenever you're ready to follow."

Rayburn turned to Staff Sergeant Mathes, the highest-ranking surviving NCO and his defacto platoon sergeant now. "Mathes, tell the guys to eat an MRE. One-to-one security until I get back."

The staff sergeant nodded in acknowledgement. "Roger that, sir."

Rayburn turned to the major who replied, "Cherie-o then, follow me."

The major led Rayburn through the fort again, and again through its menagerie of defenders. Rayburn saw the Taliban leader, who acknowledged him with a nod. Rayburn nodded in return and as the major led him they passed a partition that opened into a large space. All around was greenery and plants, a veritable garden space. The sky was open and bright. There was a large and vibrant tree in the center, one that resembled both an oak and a mangrove. Alien and beautiful. Rayburn looked around, in the middle was a large pool. It was the size of a small swimming pool, with its water bubbling up from a deep well in the middle. A spring of some sort. Rayburn saw aqueducts that led away, channeling water outside in small trenches to the walls; the source of the water that surrounded the fort.

The major motioned to a meager wooden table and a set of two chairs. Rayburn laid his rifle across the table and sat down. It was quiet and peaceful here. He found himself closing his eyes. He felt calmed and relaxed, like he could slip away into a deep sleep. He felt like there was some force here, comforting him. Making him feel safe in a sea of evil.

"Beautiful, isn't it? The garden," Major Masterson said, ripping Rayburn from his daydream. "This place, it feels magical, doesn't it?"

Rayburn nodded. "It does."

"You may have wondered why our foe hasn't tried to storm this place. It's the water." The Major motioned. "Something about it, it's magical...biblical. I don't know how to describe it, but our foe gives these waters a wide berth."

The major looked deep in thought as he stared into the deep blue that flowed forth from the spring. "You know you are immortal now?"

Rayburn looked at the major. "What are you talking about?"

"You have survived the night. That means you and your men have joined us."

"What are you talking about?" Rayburn said again, not hiding the shock on his face.

"This place, this land. Its chosen you." The major said, chuckling like this revelation was common knowledge. He sighed as he rose out of his chair and walked towards the spring. He squatted down, stretching a hand out into the water. He turned back towards Rayburn, "This valley is a blight on Earth. The land or God or whatever has invoked a response to this hell. It is contained here, so long as we defend the valley."

"I don't understand," Rayburn said flatly.

The major stared into the pool, "We've been chosen, mate. Chosen by this land or by God or by gods. Something twisted, evil, has made a nest in this place, but the powers that be have contained it here."

"So we're trapped."

"No, mate, you got it wrong. We are the defense. We've been called here, all of us. From the warriors of Alexander the Great, the hordes of Genghis Khan, to our doomed fucking selves. It's our destiny. We're here because we have fought these demons and lived to tell." He stood up, kicking the water. "We few unlucky brothers indeed."

He paused, deep in thought.

Rayburn broke the silence, "So what did you mean by *it gets easier in the morning*?"

The major turned and smiled. "You see, Lieutenant, you and your men are immortal now, just as you are now trapped in this place. You cannot *stay* dead. After you survive one night here, you will not pass on, no matter how horribly you may die." He stopped to stare at his own hand before motioning towards the water. "You see, from now on when you die. You will feel it. You will go dark and move towards the other side, towards only where the dead reside. But just before you pass those gates, you will be yanked back. Back to this place. These waters will spew your living body onto this earth...to fight again."

The major walked toward Rayburn until he stood an arm's length away. "But you won't believe me unless you see it for yourself."

Rayburn looked at him and opened his mouth in question. But he didn't see the pistol the major pulled from his holster with lighting speed.

A blast. The world was suddenly bright.

I am dead, Rayburn thought. *Or am I?*

His existence was now darkness. But he was aware of this dark; it wasn't quite oblivion like he imagined. It was like being trapped in a space of pitch darkness. He felt himself move and stumble in this dark, like he was back in a cave he remembered visiting as a child, the one when the tour guides had shut off the lights and he experienced true ad utter darkness. Then a light sparked in the distance, and he felt compelled to journey toward it. As he stepped towards the light, Rayburn felt the sensation of running water around his ankles, a water that was rising higher each second. Like a strong tide, there was a pull that then flowed away. He struggled against this tide, but it was rising and getting stronger. Soon he was lifted off his fleet and swept away from the light, floundering and flailing in the cold. Suddenly, caught as if in an undertow, he was pulled under the strange waters and shot to its surface.

He breathed violently as he suddenly awoke under that familiar tree, water clogging his lungs as he choked for air. He was back in the pool, struggling to breathe, flailing in the cool water. He felt his feet touch the ground and he struggled into the shallows. On all fours, he crawled and paddled onto the banks of the pool. Flopping onto his back he gasped for air one more time as Major Masterson peered down at him.

"I'm sorry, friend," the Major whispered, "but it was the quickest way to show you the truth."

Rayburn shook in fear, recalling his death in every detail.

"Lieutenant Rayburn, I have died more times than one can remember. You will always survive...no matter how hard you try otherwise." The old Brit, long past his span, suddenly sounded so far away, his eyes glassy and after a time he breathed. "I have been here for over three hundred years."

Rayburn rolled over onto all fours. He stared at his reflection in the water.

"It's true, Sarbaz was once my enemy. My battalion chased him into this valley and we followed into the spiders den. Much like your story. Sarbaz and his men were lucky to find the fort before the demons overwhelmed him. My battalion was not so lucky, and I was the only one to survive. All of us share the same story."

Rayburn looked at the table: where he'd been shot in the face. Somehow this was all making sense, like a voice whispering reassurances.

"When you die here," the major affirmed, "you resurrect. Your former body burns like tinder in a fire. I can't explain it, except that we have been made into phoenixes."

"Why us!?" Rayburn yelled, pulling his pistol from its holster, beginning to whimper.

Major Masterson placed a hand on the barrel of Rayburn's M9 and slowly pushed it down. "In the countless years I have spent here, I could never come up with an answer...other than Hell has broken free and this land has called us to send it back."

Rayburn looked at his pistol.

The major continued, "The valley is building an army. An army that can cleanse the blight from this land." his voice then brightened, "And maybe seal whatever hole it crawled out of."

"But," Rayburn said, rising to his feet, "now that my platoon is missing, more will come looking for us. More will get trapped here. I have to find a way to warn the others."

"There's no way you can. More will become trapped, it is true. Which is all the more reason why we have to find a way to send those bloody fuckers back to Hell. With your men, now we may actually have enough." The major smiled at Rayburn, placing both hands on his shoulders, shaking him. "I dare say, a part of me wants more of your men to arrive here—but—with whom you've already supplied, finally here, I think we can do it!"

"You do?"

Slapping Rayburn gleefully on the shoulder, he said, "Follow me."

Rayburn followed, past the hut where his men waited. He saw their looks of alarm when he walked by still dripping wet. Ssgt Mathes yelled, "Sir, are you okay? We heard a gunshot!" But Rayburn held up a hand, silently mouthing "trust me."

The major led him to a staircase at the base of a tower. Shuffling down into the dark, they entered a large hall lit with torches. The major stopped and waved his arms in excitement, "Welcome to the armory!"

And, indeed, there was reason to be excited. *How can this be?* Under the torchlight sat—waited—more weapons than a warrior could dream. Of all things, nearest Rayburn were M4 Carbines; no different than the ones he and his men carried. Beyond them, against the wall, stood dozens of spears. Boxes of ammunition were already open—waiting— along with night vision goggles and grenades spread out among other instruments of death. "Where did you find all this?" He gasped, turning to the major.

The major simply shrugged, picking up an M4. He examined the weapon. "Dunno, mate. *Magic*," he almost hissed it, his eyes alight. "Magic is all I can say." He shouldered the weapon, pointing it towards a wall. "Every new warrior brings with them something of use. Muskets, swords, bullets…they just appear here."

He handed the rifle to Rayburn. The familiar weight was comforting. The Major walked towards a large pot, overflowing with the familiar brass shapes of 5.56m NATO cartridges. "This place provides everything for us. Eternal life, food, water…eternal weapons. When I arrived here, I had three bullets, a bloody rifle, and pistol to my name. The next morning there were enough to arm a battalion."

Rayburn found himself repeated the major's earlier words. "Building an army."

Masterson picked up a pair of PVS-21 night vision

goggles and a handheld radio, scrutinizing them. "There's over three hundred of us now."

"That Neanderthal, too," Rayburn said.

The major took a step forward. Glowing under a torch's burning flame he said, "I have been here in this fort, a rat hiding or dying over and over to hide like a rat once more. But now we may have enough, enough so we can push them back into their bloody caves, back to Lucifer or Baal or whatever they call their master." He looked deep into Rayburn's eyes with a fanatical, feral look. "We. Can. Win."

PART IV

"Alright, we move out in ten!" Ssgt Mathes shouted to men packed into the courtyard. Twilight was fading and the icy howls began to fill the air. Fangs, teeth, and hate challenged the men to dare and venture into the dark.

Rayburn finished rolling up his sleeves as he looked around. His platoon hurriedly put the finishing touches on their gear as they conducted their final checks and moved into formation. He felt a hand on his shoulder. Mustafa and his entire former Taliban crew were decked out in American gear and holding M4s and RPGs. He nodded to Rayburn, and in the poor light Rayburn made out a smile.

All around him, Macedonians, Mongols, Pashtuns, Russians, and others blended in with the Americans. A Mongol warrior, draped in belts of 7.62 over his fur coat, held a M240 machine gun. A Macedonian hefted a javelin rocket launcher onto his back as the Russians tried to convince their Neanderthal companion to pick up a rifle. Their caveman friend, though, preferred a Macedonian spear.

Months of preparation had gone into this night. Countless hours of basic classes on weapons, tactics, English, and strategy. A menagerie of cultures and peoples were now one. This was the first night the Legion of the Dammed would take the fight to the Legions of Hell.

Rayburn walked up to the front as the remaining men manned the parapets with Sarbaz. They would cover the assault force from any assailants as they moved to their objective. The major met him at the front, he had traded his redcoat for a modern uniform and gear. The ancient Brit looked indistinguishable from Rayburn. "Lieutenant, are we ready to move? The lights faded and our enemy grows weary of our absence."

Rayburn keyed the radio on his kit, "Slayer7, we ready to move?"

A Russian voice prickled over the radio, "Roger, Slayer6, ready to go oscar mike. Castle6 is saying the coast is clear. They don't know what's coming for them."

Rayburn turned to the major who smiled coldly with glee, "On you then, Lieutenant." The Major turned and gave the hand signal. The large wooden doors lurched open as the

Legion rushed out. They formed up on a firing line, scanning their sectors as they had trained and drilled.

The light of the sky was all about to vanish. The small scouting parties that had been sent out in the past months had reported back the demon's positions. The men in the fort studied their foe with a zealous passion; their tactics, their weapons, how to better kill them. They had learned their foe could take a lot of damage, but the higher caliber weapons Rayburn's men and the Russians brought dispatched the demons with ease. But the demons were well organized. They had strongholds and defenses encircling the valley, but the caves to the north seemed to be where they spawned from. No doubt the Legion would have to venture into those tunnels soon. But for now, they had to cleanse the valley of as many demons as they could. They had their targets; they would cripple their enemy first before going in for biggest of kills.

Rayburn often thought about the world outside. No one had entered the valley after his platoon, and he always wondered why no one came looking for them. Maybe that guy "Barton" he'd met once knew what had happened. Maybe the power back home knew about what was happening here. Or maybe they had written them off. He wondered what the outside world had decided about his fate. And that he didn't even know what his fate would be. Would beating the demons here really release him? Would he be allowed to go home?

He pushed those thoughts out of his mind. It was time to focus. "All units on this net, Slayers are on the move." Rayburn dropped his NVGs and took the safety off his rifle. Dozens of IR lasers streamed into the night. Tonight was the beginning of the offensive.

It was time to go hunting.

COLLECTIVE

DEAD RECKONING COLLECTIVE is a veteran owned and operated publishing company. Our mission encourages literacy as a component of a positive lifestyle. Although DRC only publishes the written work of military veterans, the intention of closing the divide between civilians and veterans is held in the highest regard. By sharing these stories it is our hope that we can help to clarify how veterans should be viewed by the public and how veterans should view themselves.

Visit us at:

deadreckoningco.com

@deadreckoningcollective

@deadreckoningco

@DRCpublishing

If you enjoyed this fictional collection of stories and the premise of military paranormal encounters, then be sure to read Nick Orton's non-fictional works:

Tales From The Grid Square Stories Of Paranormal Military Experiences Volume 1
Tales From The Grid Square Volume 2: Stories Of Military Paranormal Experiences

Available on amazon.com

And be on the lookout for future collections

FOLLOW NICK ORTON
talesfromthegridsquare@gmail.com

@Tales_From_The_Gridsquare

@TFTG_Redux

@Deadlined_Art

@Tales From The Grid Square